Amber Sea of the Dead
A Kalamazoo Story

by Jason Arbogast

Red Orchid Publishing. Ankeny, IA.

### Acknowledgements

I'd like to thank everybody who finally gave in after I bugged them enough times about reading this book. In no particular order, I'd also like to thank the Iowa State University MFA program, Chris Kadolph, Tom Gartin for the interior illustrations and layout, editor Adam Nelson, cover artist Jon Hammond, and my publisher Melanny Henson.

**For Grandpa and Grandma**

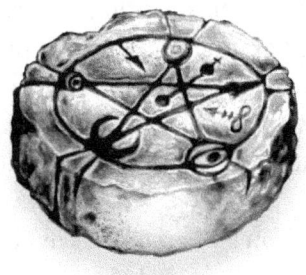

## 1.

Kalamazoo. Say it. What does it make you think of? Maybe rolling hills covered in trees as thick as time. Or a mist-covered valley or two, filled with busy industry. If you're particularly imaginative, you might think it sounds like something out of a fairy tale. And you'd be right. Kalamazoo has trees hidden away in it that remember the arrival of the first dark-skinned Americans. Businesses fill the valleys the town was built in, but not everyone is ready, or able, to see places like the Forgotten Bar, stuck between real Kalamazoo and imagined Kalamazoo. It has monsters, and a few heroes, too, like any fairy tale. But mostly it has the blood. Because Kalamazoo is an old story, from when fairy tales were there to warn people of the things that'd happen to you if you were foolish enough to talk to strangers or to go off the path. Kalamazoo is a reminder that, no matter what people think, the old things in woods, with their sharpened teeth and bloodied claws, still live out there. Some of them might have put on human faces, but they still want nothing more than to pull you off of the trail and into the darkness so they can suck your skin hollow and wear your life until they find another victim.

Don't get me wrong. Lots of people like Kalamazoo, myself included once upon a time. It has a lot to recommend itself: two very good colleges, many great coffee-shops, various festivals over the summer, and an amazing night-life. If you're lucky, you'll live in the town all your life and that's all you'll see of it, because most travel brochures don't mention that Kalamazoo is also one of the biggest playgrounds for supernatural things in existence. If enough people worshipped, feared, or just plain believed in it, it's made its way through town at one point. This means more ghosts, supernatural critters, and inhuman things taking up residence in just about every nook, cranny, and sewer than you can shake a Ouija board at. It also means booming sales in New Age paraphernalia. It was probably one of the idiot New Agers who gave Kalamazoo the nickname Kazoo. Their kind like things quick and easy, preferably with incense, which is why I wind up cleaning up one of their messes and the bloody smear they've left on the walls at least once a week.

My name's Roger. Don't worry about my last name. It's only important to me. What is important is that I'm Kalamazoo's Detective, a sort of supernatural peacekeeper and straightener of mystical messes. I have a "gift" that lets me see and sense supernatural things. More of a curse, really. There's a reason people can't see what's really right in front of them. Little thing called staying sane. But I use it to try and keep the city, and sometimes its people if I get lucky, safe from the old things that everybody thinks, and hopes, are gone. Sometimes, though, cases come up that surprise even me. Like helping a god die back in November of 2002 and all the crap that came after it.

In my seven years as Kalamazoo's Detective, I'd seen and done just about every kind of random paranormal cliché you could think of. Some bored or lonely god trying to end the world? Loki tried it last week. Indra a month before that. Vampires? Nice little community of them on the local college campus. Their leader and his girlfriend are pals of mine. Time travelers? Got one of them that hangs out at the coffee shop just down the street from my office. He's not always the most stable guy, but he's all right when he's sober. And don't get me started on the damn faeries in Bronson Park.

Assisted deicide, on the other hand, was something else. I'd killed a few gods, of course. Part of the job, and they usually got better. But I'd never helped one go willingly.

The goddess Vesta had come to me to find a dignified way to end her life. Her Vestal Virgins long gone, most of her worshippers dead for centuries, and her function as goddess of the hearth and home made irrelevant in the modern world, she was seeking a way out that was as quiet and as peaceful as herself. Normally, I disliked gods and their haughty attitudes toward humans. Name a bad trait and any random god had it. But not Vesta. Her quiet strength was always enough. The one time that I'd run into her before, she seemed more like the cool, unmarried aunt everyone had who let you get away with anything, but you were never rude enough to try it because you didn't want to disappoint her.

And now I had to find a way to kill her. She'd asked me to meet her in Bronson Park to talk about the situation. Bronson Park, with five churches on three of its sides, the ghost of another on its fourth[1] , the Crypt of the Future some fifty feet below the ground, and the Church of the Lost Moon hidden in the clouds a few hundred feet up, would have qualified as the most sacred location in the city if it weren't for the small Faerie mound in its northwest corner. It didn't necessarily profane the park, but it definitely dirtied the place up.

We were sitting by the Fountain of the Pioneers, drained for the winter. The hideous thing always made me think of a garbage scow, with its unnecessary tower of concrete[2] jutting up like a rudder from behind its pock-marked, rectangular basin. The layer of coins littering the basin in the warmer months, giving it the sparkle of deep water, only added to the effect. However, ugly it was, it marked the location of Kalamazoo's first home, making it the ideal place for us to meet.

"Are you sure you want to do this?" I asked, shoving my hands in my trench coat's pockets to keep from fidgeting and revealing my discomfort at the whole situation. "You've probably got enough power left to last a few more centuries before you fade out. And you don't have enough believers left to come back if you change your mind."

Since Rome had fallen, Vesta had been considerably lacking in the belief department, and for a god belief is the name of the game. The more followers they have, and the stronger those followers believe in them, the stronger the god becomes. With enough belief fueling them, a god could do whatever miracle you name. Water into wine? Simple. Raze a city? You got it. Resurrection? It's a biggie, but not impossible.

A warm, late autumn breeze, ruined by the burning chemical smell of the paper mill to the east, blew a lock of Vesta's long, black hair into her face. Silver streaked it in a few places. She brushed it away and smiled at me. Dimples appeared in her olive-colored cheeks. For just a moment, I had that warm ball of pride in my chest that you get when you're a kid and your mom tells you that you did a great job on something.

"I was in Charlotte, North Carolina, a few months ago, Roger. Have

[1] The only Methodist church that I knew of where midnight and three a.m. masses were the norm. Its trustees had put their hearts and souls into getting it built back in the 1860s, literally in the case of one guy, so it burning to the ground in the twenties meant it just switched congregations.

[2] A stylized pioneer and Native American close enough to kiss, except that the pioneer towers over the Native American, rifle at attention, looking for all the world like he's about to bludgeon the other guy to death. As metaphors go, it's less than subtle.

3

you been there?"

"No. Never really had a reason to."

"It's nice. You should go sometime. Personally, I love the South. They still know how important family is there. There's always someone who'll invite you over to talk about their kin over some iced tea or lemonade."

"Sounds perfect for you."

"It is. But it won't last much longer. Internet, satellite TV, and the rest will see to that."

"I don't know about that," I said.

"I do. It's important to know your time, Roger. And mine's up."

The simple honesty in her voice, along with its obvious pain, convinced me more than the words could. I took a hand out my pocket and rested it on one of hers. "I wish the other gods had your sense. Give me a day. Do what you need to, talk to whoever you need to, and then give me a call around five. We'll go from there."

I got up and started walking away.

"Thank you," she said to me.

I turned, trying not to show any emotion that might upset her. Her constant smile nearly cracked my neutral expression, nearly made me show how guilty the whole situation was making me feel. The smile made her face, which appeared middle-aged but in fact had never appeared anything but, look so trusting and sure of its purpose. I was reminded for a moment of the final scene from *Of Mice and Men*.

I returned the smile with a warmth that the years as Detective had taught me to fake. "I'm just doing my job," I told her. I turned and walked away without looking back.

"Poor Detective," a voice gargled at me from the fountain's drains as I left. "Gets to kill another god, and he's all weepy about it. Grow a spine, boy."

"Shut up, River," I said without stopping.

The spirit of the Kalamazoo River and I had never gotten along. Like many water spirits, it hated humanity for polluting the hell out of it, which meant that it was almost always on the side of anything trying to kill us all off. For my part, I hated it for turning my shower water into a septic sludge on a regular basis

As I left the park, laughter like the sound of an asphyxiating child followed. Which worried me. The river in a good mood never meant anything good, for me or for humanity in general.

*          *          *          *

I sat at a stop sign, tapping the steering wheel to the beat of the rain that had started after I left the park. Most people would've just chalked rain after a death request from a friend up to coincidence, but most people didn't have my on-the-job experience. I was trying to figure out if I needed a coffee or a drink, leaning hard toward the drink thanks to the rain's nudge of my mood. Then I noticed the utburd crawling down the sidewalk. One windshield wiper swish there was nothing, and the next a blue and naked little girl making her way down the sidewalk on all fours and oblivious to the rain, her umbilical cord still attached.

There are three basic reasons that a ghost hangs on: they don't know they're dead, they have unfinished business, or they just don't want to move on. Powered by rage, utburds fall into the second category. Pitiful and nasty things, they're the ghosts of children murdered by their parents, and they usually only stick around so that they can kill the parent they think is responsible for their death. Luckily, it was rare that I had to deal with one, but when I did it usually left me feeling the need for a drink for the next week. They never moved on easily, which meant that I was forced to do things that I'd rather not to something that looked like a kid.

Another utburd, also a girl, materialized. This one, wearing a dirty set of pink overalls, was about three years old and had a partially collapsed skull, grey matter and splinters of bone nearly hidden by a brown ponytail tied off with a pink ribbon. She carefully lifted the younger one up, then looked at me with pale eyes. The windshield wiper swished by her, and she was gone.

"Ah damn. Suzie's back." I sighed. "This day just keeps getting better and better."

Little Suzie was only technically an utburd. She'd been out with the family for a drive back in the eighties and died when some drunk ran a red light and T-boned the family car. Her father was driving, though, so her ghost stuck around to get revenge on him. Must've been pretty angry when she found out he'd died in the accident, making it kind of tough for her to kill him. Since then, she'd decided to stay around and help any other utburds that popped up to kill whoever they were after.

I'd been meaning to take care of Suzie for the past few years but had managed to keep finding excuses not to. On the one hand, she and her playmates were just kids and really weren't to blame for what had happened

5

to them. On the other hand, they were powerful spirits of vengeance that just wanted to kill people. The fact that the people they were after most likely deserved it wasn't really my call.

I put on my turn signal and headed west.

*      *      *      *

Several bad places exist in Kalamazoo. Only natural, I suppose, when you got things setting up shop that'd scared the hell out of people as an occupation for the better part of recorded history. OP Avenue's Wight Halls, Bronson Park's Folded Woods, and Mountain Home - the massive, rolling cemetery sitting across from Kalamazoo College that looked like it was about to explode or give birth (to what is a question that's kept me up more nights than I like admitting. Especially after the Cult of Cleaver episode) to name a few. Less than ten minutes after spotting Suzie, I was standing on the sidewalk beside one of the worst places in the city: Kiddy-Time Day Care. Well, the remains of it, anyway. Kiddy-Time had been forced to close down about ten years back when some disturbing rumors had popped up about things the staff members were doing with the kids in the basement. Most of the rumors, mainly the sexual ones, weren't true, but some of the others were, like the ones involving demon worship: this gave the place the feeling of a spiritual sewage dump and made my soul feel like it was coated in oil every time I passed by. Made it the perfect haunt for ghosts with nothing but anger to keep them going.

I stared at the crumbling, one-story building, getting up the courage to go in. I've seen and done some pretty nasty things in my career as Detective, but not much matched Kiddy-Time for sheer wrongness. It almost passed the cemetery in that department. The building's yellow paint, probably bright and cheerful in its prime, had chipped and faded to a color closer to a jaundice victim's skin. Somehow, the two windows framing the dry-rotted front door were still intact, bright and clear, shiny like the eyes of the dying. The orange half-light of the streetlamps didn't help, either. It just made the place seem even more unreal, like some sort of fever dream. Probably the worst thing, though, was the playground surrounding the place. Glistening metal equipment that should have turned brown with rust years ago and shiny plastic swings that should have rotted away into unrecognizability sat on cracked, dead earth. Whether this was Suzie's fault or the result of whatever the daycare's staff had done, I couldn't say, but not much is as

6

unnatural as an undead playground.

Except maybe an undead playground filled with about twenty dead children at night. As I watched, the ghosts of children ranging from newborn to probably six began appearing on the equipment, flaring into sight like little blue candle flames. Most weren't visibly damaged, but a few made it difficult for even me to look at. I expected to see adults with knife wounds or charred bodies, not children.

The kids went through the motions of playing on the equipment, but none of the babies giggled as older kids pushed them on the swings, no one smiled on the way down the slide, and none of the kids on the merry-go-round so much as laughed.

At least the rain had let up for the moment.

"This is way above my pay grade," I said under my breath.

"Hi, Detective," a girl said to me from about waist level.

I put on my best smile and looked down.

"Hi, Suzie. Some nice friends you've got there."

She shrugged. "They're okay."

"Just okay?"

"Yeah. They're always asking me what to do next. I don't like it. I'm just a kid. I don't want to be in charge."

I slipped my right hand into one of my trench coat's pockets. "I hope that's not a job offer, because I've already got one."

"But after we kill you, you won't be Detective anymore," she said reasonably, "and you can take care of us forever, and I won't be in charge anymore."

I glanced up at the playground. All of the kids had stopped what they were doing. Forty dead eyes stared at me.

I looked back down at Suzie.

"True, but I'm not ready to die just yet. Sorry kid."

"But if we kill you now, the snakes won't eat you."

That got my attention. Humanity had had quite the love/hate relationship with snakes over the millennia, meaning the list of evil snake and snake-like things out there could just about fill a book. Damballa sprang immediately to mind after what he did during the War of Storms, but he'd been banished from the city. Hekate was a possibility, since no one had heard from her in a couple years, but so were Eastern dragons, Lamia, and any number of things.

"What snakes, Suzie?" I asked in my most kid-friendly voice.

"The walking ones." Suzie held out her hands like they were claws and started stomping around making hissing noises.

I had a hunch about this but hoped I was wrong.

"Suzie, were these snakes really tall?" I held my hand up at about seven feet. "Looked kind of like people?"

She stopped playing walking snake and looked at me. "They don't like you. They told us not to kill you, though. Said they'd eat us if we did."

"That doesn't sound very nice."

"It's not. We loved Jimmy, and one of them ate him to prove they weren't lying." The sidewalk cracked under her. "And it's your fault."

"Settle down, Suzie."

"I hate you!" she shouted and jumped at me, hands outstretched.

"Susan Marie Hollings," I said just before her hands reached my throat.

Suzie disappeared.

I pulled a twitching, pink urinal cake out of my pocket, bringing with it the smell of antiseptic. A faint circle lined with various mystic symbols decorated it, making it look like a magical hockey puck. I kept a couple of them on me at all times just in case, pissed off ghosts being a sort of occupational hazard. Great things, urinal cakes. Soft enough to be carved on, embarrassing enough that no ghost wanted to be stuck in one. The ritual was simple enough, too. Just a basic summoning, really, with the urinal cake acting like a mini summoning circle. All they needed to go off was for me to say the name of whoever I wanted to stick in them.

"You need a time out, little girl," I told Suzie in her new home.

The ground shook, reminding me of two things. One, the small army of dead children now walking, crawling, and toddling toward me, rage contorting their faces into things that were only passingly human. And two, the reason why utburds were so dangerous. The way they killed their victims was to sit on the person's chest, growing heavier and heavier, until they crushed them. I'd seen the body of one guy whose dead son had come back for him. Looked like a five-hundred pound weight had dropped on him from twenty feet up. Even the bed I'd found him in was broken.

I searched one of my trench coat's left pockets for something to use against them. All I found was a small bezoar and a saint's pinky bone, both of which were completely useless against ghosts. Having nowhere near enough urinal cakes on me to handle that many ghosts, I did the only responsible thing I could do: I ran for my car.

The ground continued shaking as the utburds marched slowly after me. In the distance, a car alarm went off from the vibrations, then another, and another, until electronic wails and beeps filled the air.

I opened the passenger's side door on my red '89 Sunbird and jumped in, slamming it shut behind me. I tossed Suzie in her new, antiseptic home into the back seat, then yanked the tape off of the car's broken glove compartment and began rooting through the collection of random objects I'd tossed in there over the years.

By the time I finally found what I was looking for, the stub of a poorly rolled cigar, the kids were at my door. A few at the front of the horde tried to just walk through it and bounced off. I smiled. A few years back, I'd cornered Papa Legba, the voodoo god of comings and goings, and gotten him to seal my car off from anything I didn't want entering it. The look of surprise that flashed through their anger gave me a brief surge of hope that I might make it out of this one. Then the larger ones began lifting the smaller ones onto the roof. The wards that Papa Legba had put up could take the spiritual weight, but I wasn't so sure the car could take the physical weight.

The roof groaned in answer to my question.

I pushed in the cigarette lighter and watched as more utburds were boosted onto the roof.

What seemed like an eternity passed until the lighter popped out. I grabbed it and lit my cigar as fast as I could, making sure not to inhale any of the green smoke that began billowing out from it.

The reaction of the utburds was immediate. The ones old enough to speak said things like, "Ew, gross!" and, "Sick!" and backed away. The utburds on the roof crawled off and thudded onto the ground with as much speed as their short legs could give them, most of them crying.

One of the paradoxes of ghosts that I'd probably never understand was that, despite having no need to breathe, they had a heightened sense of smell. Especially strong smells could keep even the most determined of spirits away. And my cigars had a smell strong enough to melt nosehairs.

I took a moment to calm down, then opened my car's door and stepped out.

The kids had formed up, with the taller ones lined up in front of the smaller ones. Most of them were pinching their noses to keep the smell of my cigar out. It didn't seem to be working, though, because as I moved forward, they moved back.

"Give us Suzie back!" a boy with no visible wounds demanded.

9

"You're not exactly in a position to be giving me orders, kid."

He smiled in that way smart-assed kids who think they know everything do.

"That's what you think."

He began stomping on the ground in the "shave and a haircut" rhythm. Stomp, stompstompstompstomp, stomp, stomp. The others soon picked it up, shaking the ground again and causing the daycare's windows to rattle in time. STOMP, STOMPSTOMPSTOMPSTOMP, STOMP, STOMP.

I was about to tell them to knock it off when I sensed something move just below the daycare. One of the more useful parts of my "gift" lets me feel where ghosts and most supernatural things are once they manifest. Usually this amounts to nothing more than my arm or neck hairs tingling and a feeling of being watched from that direction. But this was something else. This was the feeling a mouse gets just before an owl rips it into the air. The feeling that cavemen got when the sun went down and the wolves started rustling in the forest just beyond the firelight.

A demon.

I'd had encounters with demons before. Generally, I got along with them, since they had an honesty to them that gods usually didn't. They were evil and out to steal your soul, but at least you knew where you stood with a demon. Gods had more of a penchant for mystery than most demons, and you could never really tell if they were trying to help or hinder you. You could always count on a demon to be trying to hinder you. And I could respect that kind of duplicitous honesty.

Most of them, anyway. There were a few, less civilized demons left over from older, more primal times that couldn't care less about souls or anything so esoteric. They simply wanted everything dead, preferably after a good, long hunt involving several shallow, yet bloody, cuts. This one felt like the kill-everything variety as it ripped its way up into the real world.

I thought about making a break for my car, but the thing would probably just follow me and wait for me to get out.

The daycare darkened, as if it and the piece of reality it occupied were fading from the world or something more real were moving forward, outshining the flimsy piece of three-dimensional space around it. That something turned out to be a wolf about the size of a pony with black, matted fur striding out of the darkness, its gaze fixed firmly on me. As it got closer, I saw a snake's tail curling lazily behind it, grey scales glistening in a light that didn't exist here. Something in my genes told me to run and not look back. I ignored it, but just barely.

"You're not scaring me with the whole snake-wolf thing, you know," I lied. "So put on your human face."

It laughed and my soul flinched. The utburds wavered like images on a bad TV. "Detective," it growled. "So nice to finally meet you."

"Wish I could say the same. What's your name?"

It sat among the utburds, about five feet away from me. Occasionally, its tail would twitch. "And why should I tell you that?"

I forced out a smile. "Professional courtesy?"

It laughed again, making me regret the joke. "No."

I reached into a pocket and pulled out the saint's pinky bone and pointed it at the demon. "Fine, we'll do this the old way. By the power of Saint Lazarus, I command you to tell me your name."

It cocked its head as if thinking. "The painter? You couldn't even muster up a respectable saint to confront me with? I should eat your soul just for that."

"Heaven forbid if I've offended you. I wasn't exactly planning on fighting a demon tonight. Now, name?"

It sighed. "Amon."

"Any relation to the god?"

"No."

I knew it was a bad idea to poke the horrific source of evil, but I couldn't resist. It wasn't like it could kill me twice. "Never heard of you."

It stood and bared its double rows of pointed teeth. "I am Amon, demon of rage, Marquis of Hell, commander of forty-four legions. I have devoured the souls of emperors."

"You and every other demon."

Which was true. Hell gave out the title of marquis like it was candy on Halloween and legions like farms gave out kittens.

I was on the ground without even seeing Amon move. His teeth, remarkably white, were less than an inch from my face. The rotten-egg smell of sulfur mixed with the metallic scent of congealed blood engulfed me, bringing tears to my eyes. I like to think it was the smell, anyway.

"You are fortunate, Detective, that your services are needed elsewhere this evening. If you were not ending the world soon…"

And he was back among the utburds, sitting perfectly at ease as if he'd never moved.

"Now leave," Amon told me as I got up. "Kill humanity for me."

Some people might be worried when a demon seems so certain they're going to bring about the end of the world. I'll admit that I was a little concerned, but not overly. Ever since taking over as Kalamazoo's Detective, I'd prevented the end of the world at least twenty times. Some form of apocalypse was about to happen, or predicted to happen, or destined to happen at least twice a year, sometimes three times. My causing it was a unique twist, but still not enough to make my boots shake.

"Amon," the boy who'd summoned him whined. "Kill him. He's got Suzie."

The demon looked at the boy, then promptly bit his head off. The utburd's body tottered for a moment, then faded away like smoke.

"You'd better hope I do end it," I said to the demon. "Because if I don't, I'm coming back here to knock you back to Hell."

"Of course you will."

He turned and walked back to the daycare center, unconcerned. After a long glare at me, the utburds faded away, one by one.

I wasn't sure whether to put this one in the win or loss column, so I just shrugged and headed back for my car. I was still alive, which counted as a win, I suppose, if not a particularly satisfying one. But sometimes you have to take what you can get in a business where even death isn't always permanent.

*     *     *     *

There are any number of ways to kill a god. They range from the overly theatric, with destined weapons, heroes of virtue, and whatever other Wagnerian theme you might think of, to the very basic blunt object to the head. Oh, the blunt object would probably have to be made of silver or some other holy or unholy material, but it all boiled down to an old-fashioned beating. Gods don't go quietly. Too in love with the idea that the world can't go on without them, even if it's done so just fine for centuries, in some cases millennia. Which was why Vesta's willing death would have to require something special. Something fitting for a goddess of the family.

My encounter the previous day with the utburds gave me an idea for the perfect exit.

At six o'clock, I took Vesta to Bronson Hospital's neo-natal room, up on the fourth floor. Babies lay on blue and pink blankets, some sleeping with their thumbs in their mouths, others with little balled-up fists waving back and forth as they cried for their mothers, or possibly to return to the warmth they'd recently been separated from. Each one's bed was numbered.

We watched all this from the other side of a huge plastic window for a moment. For that moment, my cynical little heart felt a surge of hope for the future. I quickly reminded it why we were there, and it went back to beating with contempt for the world.

"Thank you," Vesta told me.

"Just doing my job, dear. But before you go, do you want to tell me what really happened to convince you it's your time? Hate for you to go out on a lie."

I'd had time to think over what Vesta was asking me and why. Sure, it was possible that she really was that pessimistic about the future of the family, but I doubted it. Gods never told the truth when a lie worked so much better. In Vesta's case, I was inclined to believe she was doing it out of some form of motherly need to protect me from a harsh truth, but still...

"I was walking through a neighborhood down in Charlotte when John waved me over, saying it was too hot for a pretty lady to be walking around."

Vesta touched my forehead. A moment of vertigo and I was in her memory, standing next to her.

"Where is everybody today?" Vesta asked John, the elderly man sitting across from her in a white suit.

They were at a blue table with a glass top on John's daughter's front porch. Looking around, Vesta could see several other houses, all with empty front porches and neatly trimmed, empty yards.

John's hand shook a little as he picked up his glass of iced tea and took a drink, causing the screened-in porch to temporarily sound like a craps table. "Inside," he said as he shakily put the glass down. "Out of the heat. Pansies."

She smiled at this, bringing out the laugh lines that decorated her middle-aged face.

"You probably don't remember this, but back in my time, a day like this wouldn't of been nothing. We'd of been out playing or picnicking or what have you. Little heat like this weren't nothing."

Vesta pointed to one of the grey strands of hair in her black hair. "Hey, I've earned these. I remember."

"Pretty young thing like you?" he asked, a lop-sided smile coming to his face. "You're what, thirty-five? Forty?"

13

Vesta picked up her lemonade. "I'm a little older than that, but I appreciate the compliment," she said before taking a sip.

"Do you remember the sixties?" John asked.

Vesta nodded.

"Awful times," John went on. "Damn hippies everywhere. Even Janice," he nodded toward the house, "burned her bra for some fool reason. Once the sixties hit, it all went to hell."

"They weren't that bad. People were starting to do what made them happy instead of what they thought they had to do."

He waved her off with a frail hand. "Bah. They learned to be layabouts who didn't know what a good day's work was. Not like in the fifties. We all worked then, and everything was good. Our kids listened to us and loved us."

Vesta's voice sounded from somewhere in my head. "I felt a bit of belief coming from John and decided to try and draw out more. It had become so hard to know when I'd find more…"

"What do you mean?" the Vesta at the table asked John.

His face softened as he remembered. "Every night, they begged for a story and a kiss from me. And every afternoon they'd run to the door and hug my legs when I got home."

"Sounds nice."

"I'd give anything for that again," he said quietly.

A voice came from the house. "Papa? Where are you?" It was a little girl's.

John looked quickly over to the house, which had changed from his daughter's white two-story to a brown single level. "Janice?"

"Papa, you're home!" the little girl shouted. There was the sound of small, quick steps on linoleum.

John stood as fast as his old body would let him. "I'm home, honey." He shuffled to the screen door.

Vesta watched, and basked in the flow of belief that was coming from him, redirecting it into maintaining the illusion.

"The belief wasn't in me, as such," she said from off-stage, "but in one of the things that I embodied. It wasn't terribly powerful, just enough to remind me of how diminished I'd become since the glory years, when hundreds of thousands of people had believed in me."

Vesta looked at the houses across the street.

"I thought, 'Charlotte has over a million people in it. I could do something like this on a larger scale, going neighborhood to neighborhood, gaining belief as I go. I might even be able to become stronger than I'd been before.'"

She glanced at John. Tears were running down his face as he stood wrapped in the illusion she had created. She stopped.

"I'd become like the other gods for a moment, greedy and concerned only with my survival. I'd hurt John without caring what it did to him."

Vesta looked down in shame. "John, come sit back down."

He did so mechanically.

"Wipe your tears and forget what just happened."

He did.

She looked up, faking a smile. "It happens to everybody. Kids have to grow up. Everything has to end some time."

"Yeah, I know," he said as they picked up the earlier conversation without him knowing they'd ever left it. "But it's tough. Those were good times."

"That's what grandkids are for. You get to play with them and then get rid of them when they get on your nerves. Or so I'm told."

John chuckled. "You got that right."

They sat quietly for a moment.

"Well, I've got to get going, John," Vesta said as she stood. "It's been nice chatting with you."

He stood up slowly. "Where're you off to in such a rush? Still plenty of daylight left."

She smiled apologetically. "I know, but I just realized I've got to head up to Kalamazoo to talk to a friend and take care of some business."

"That's that place up in Michigan, ain't it?"

"Yeah. How do you know about it?"

John started shuffling, vaguely dancing. "The song. I've got a gaaal, in Kalamazoo zoo zoo." He sang the last part.

Vesta laughed loudly, putting her hand in front of her mouth. She went over to John and hugged him. "You take care."

He hugged her back. "You too. Come back so I can tell you about how the wife and I met."

"I'd love that," she said truthfully, then followed it up with a lie. "I'll be back soon."

They let go of each other.

"Can't wait," he said.

The vision ended.

"Family isn't about using each other like that," she said, the same look of shame on her face. "It's about helping each other."

As much as I hate being drawn into visions without warning, I just didn't have the heart to be my normal, surly self at her. Instead, I put a hand on her shoulder. "It's all right. You did the right thing."

She managed a smile that I almost believed. "Thanks."

"Any last words?"

"Watch out for snakes."

My confusion must have shown on my face because she laughed at me, covering her mouth with a hand to hide the genuine smile that appeared at my expense.

"Interesting last words. Don't think they're the ones I would've gone with, but they are memorable, I suppose."

"I know you're not that dense, Roger. It's a prophecy."

I rolled my eyes. Prophecies always annoyed the piss out of me. Usually, they only made sense after the event they predicted, making them pretty worthless. Even with what Suzie had said the day before, it really didn't help me in any way I could see. "Could you be a little more specific?"

"Nope. Sorry. It doesn't work that way."

I sighed, then gently told her, "All right. Pick a baby and tell me what its home is like."

Serious now, Vesta pointed at one. "Number three has only one parent now. Her dad was killed last week when the driver of a car lost control and jumped the sidewalk. She'll grow up in a house filled with sadness because her mother won't be able to get over his death."

"Will she be happy?" I prompted.

Vesta shook her head. "No. Her mother just sees her as a reminder of her husband."

"Fix it. Give her the knowledge that someone out there loves her and that she'll find them."

Vesta nodded. A little more of her hair lightened to grey, and I noticed some small wrinkles appearing around her eyes.

"Pick another."

We did this for two more babies, giving them something to hope for, to hold on to, to keep in their hearts despite whatever their home lives told them. By the fourth, Vesta could barely stand as osteoporosis hunched her over and old age weakened her legs.

We'd also acquired a young couple ooing and ahhing at their baby.

"Which one's yours?" the new mother asked, smiling.

"None of them," I replied. "I'm just here to help my friend die."

"Number twelve is ours," the new father pointed to a sleeping baby in a pink blanket, ignoring what I said.

Gotta love new parents. The only thing in their world is their precious darling. Not that it mattered much. The average person's mind was about as capable of accepting the supernatural as my ex-girlfriend was of admitting that she was wrong. Sure, it was theoretically possible, but the likelihood of it came close to nil. Their minds just weren't wired that way. Probably for the best. I sure as hell wish I didn't have to live with half of the things I've seen.

I got back to work.

"Pick another," I said, knowing that we were almost finished and hating myself for what I was causing to happen, in spite of what small good it would bring.

"Number eighteen has a family that loves him, but he won't get to see them."

"Why not?" I asked, looking at the little boy.

The baby stopped moving.

"Because he just stopped breathing." With that, Vesta disappeared. The few pieces of jewelry she'd been wearing fell tinkling to the floor, and her clothes crumpled into a pile.

The boy in bed number eighteen started wailing.

"Leave it to the Romans to come up with a better god," I said, shaking my head a little.

"Where'd your mother go?" the new father asked, looking everywhere but the floor.

"Home," I said, letting some hope slip into my voice.

After a minute, I turned and walked away, leaving the clothes behind me. One more death on my conscience in the name of my job and Kalamazoo. Just another day as Detective.

2.

Half an hour later, I stood outside the door to my ground floor apartment, under the stairs and just out of the way of the occasional spray of rain that the wind tried to shower me with, mentally preparing myself for what waited inside. Finally, I opened the door, ignoring the eviction notice taped to it. The money would show up somehow. It always did.

Words like squalid and filthy would start a person on the road to a proper adjective to describe my apartment, but they'd fall far short. Stepping up to the compound adjectives, like pigsty and cesspool, you'd be getting a little closer. In the end, the best word you could probably come up with would be funky. Rancid milk, my God what is that smell and which pile of things is it coming from sort of funky. But it was necessary. The smell was the only way I knew of to keep all but the most desperate of ghosts out of my apartment.

"Dammit," I said as I stepped into the apartment, shaking the water off myself.

I'd kind of been in a rush when I'd left to help Vesta, so I'd accidentally left the closet door near the apartment's entrance open. It's nearness to the front door meant that it was a little less rank than the rest of the apartment, so instead of being greeted by the closed, white, metal door, I was greeted by the corpse of a woman, purple-faced, swollen-tongued, and bulging-eyed, hanging from the metal rod by a white sheet. The crimson stripper outfit, essentially a ruffled bra and panties, lent an unexpected twist to the grotesqueness.

"I'm not impressed," I said, taking down a coat hanger and then putting my trench coat next to the corpse. "About five years ago I got to see a pestilence spirit pull itself together out of corpse parts so rotted they were almost liquid, and on that scale you don't even make a blip."

She didn't say anything.

"You know," I continued, "I'd really appreciate it if this could wait until later. I've had kind of a rough couple of days and would really like to just go to bed."

Normally I'm a night person. Part of the job. But, in addition to the Vesta thing and dealing with the utburds, I'd had to take care of two hauntings pretty early in the morning. And, like an amateur, I'd decided to make the rounds instead of doing the sensible thing and taking a nap. It all took its toll after a while. Besides, how likely was it that I'd cause the end of the world from bed?

The woman obstinately continued to hang there.

I shrugged and closed the apartment and closet doors. Taking big, deliberate steps in order to avoid tripping over some of the larger piles of assorted things on the floor that the darkness was hiding, I headed to my bedroom.

I almost made it when I heard a hoarse, female voice nearby say, "Please, help me."

I dropped my head and slowly put my foot on the floor, resigning myself to a long, bed-free night that might bring about the end of the world. I lifted the foot again experimentally to make sure the floor would give it back while I figured out what to do about the woman. It came up with some effort.

I turned around to face the general area of darkness that it felt like she was in.

"I'm going to take a shot in the dark here," I winced internally at this unintended pun, "and guess that you didn't commit suicide."

"Someone killed me," she said quietly, as if afraid that her murderer would hear.

"And, because it can never be that simple, you don't know who did it."

Crying was my only answer.

After sighing heavily, I started walking to the living room, tripping over a couple of small piles of garbage or clothes, I couldn't quite tell which. Eventually, I found the couch and sat down. I turned on the table lamp next to it. The woman stood two feet away from me, tears trickling sideways over waxen flesh. Her broken neck made her head lie at an odd angle on her shoulder, giving her the impression of an eternally perplexed zombie. I turned the light off.

"Could you fix that, please?" I said flatly. "I'm not going to talk to you looking like that."

She began crying harder. "How?" she asked miserably between sobs.

I'll be the first to admit that I'm an ass. I'll gladly be cruel and heartless to just about anyone and anything, living, dead, or otherwise, that I feel the need to be cruel and heartless to, and the night was turning into the kind that would put most of the planet into that category. But I do have one fatal vulnerability, for my job anyway: women crying. Especially pretty ones. I always chalked it up to bad genes, if just for my own peace of mind. Normally this wasn't a problem, since most ghosts were about as attractive as road kill, and even fewer of the people who had problems with them were much better. I had a hunch, though…

"Rule number one: Being dead's mostly a mental thing. Just think of how you usually look, and you'll look like that."

I waited a moment. "Ready for the light?"

"I think so."

I turned on the light and my suspicions were confirmed. In place of the hanged woman was a pretty stripper in a skin-tight, red leather corset-looking thing that left just enough to the imagination to be provocative. I was a little surprised that she was only pretty, as opposed to the beautiful or, more frequently, trashy that I expected strippers to be, and a little alarmed. I could deal with beautiful women. I just ignored them, like they tended to ignore me, or acted like an ass toward them. Whichever was appropriate for the situation. Pretty women offered another challenge altogether. They were, theoretically, in my league, so I'd sometimes forget myself and act human toward them. And, with shoulder-length blond hair and a roundish face dominated by a slightly crooked nose, she was definitely pretty.

She clapped her hands together and jumped up a few inches in delight, causing her pert little breasts to jiggle some. "It worked!" She spun around and looked at herself. "I'm me again!"

"No, you're part of you," I said, trying to maintain my professional detachment in the face of extreme odds and perky body parts. "The rest of you is either still hanging somewhere in its bra and panties or waiting to be autopsied right now."

The woman deflated a little and began to fade. "I'm sorry."

I rolled my eyes. "Stop with the pity attempts for a moment. If you want my help, you need to stay here all the way and not try to play me like one of your johns."

Her eyes got big and she strode up to me, getting more and more solid all the while. She tried to slap me with one of her intangible hands, nearly losing her balance and tumbling into me when her hand passed through me.

I smiled, enjoying the show the same way I did every other time a ghost tried to hit me. The entertainment was worth the icy sensation her hand brought with it. "Rule number two: You can't touch things. The only thing that keeps you from sinking into the center of the planet is that you're used to not falling through the ground." This wasn't entirely true, but I really didn't feel the need to go into too much detail for someone who'd hopefully be leaving soon.

"Anything else?" she said angrily as she quickly regained her balance. Job experience, I figured.

"I'll tell you as things come up. Fresh out of 'So You're A Ghost' brochures at the moment."

"They make those?"

"No. And even if they did I couldn't afford to have any."

I sighed. "Might as well get this started. What's the last thing you remember?"

I doubted this would get me any information I needed, but you never knew. Usually, the answer amounted to something like, "I was doing something, then I woke up dead." If the universe was feeling especially hateful toward me, they woke up dead in my apartment. Took me four years to figure out that this was because whatever in Kalamazoo had picked me to be its Detective was sending them to me.

She thought for a moment. "I was at work. Then everything went dark, and I woke up in your closet."

"Of course. What's the date?" I needed to know how long she'd been dead. It'd let me know if I was going to have to deal with cops wherever she'd died, and if I'd have to pull some strings to eventually see the body.

"November third," she said with some annoyance. "What's that got to do with anything?"

"Today's the tenth. You've been gone for a while." I held up a hand. "And no, before you ask, I don't know why it took you a week to materialize."

I rubbed my eyes. I was going to need coffee if I expected to stay awake for this. "Does the last place you remember being have coffee? You may not have noticed it, but I'm a little tired to be investigating wrongful deaths. Some caffeine would go a long way toward fixing that."

Anger crossed her face again, but she contained herself. "Sorry if my death inconvenienced you."

"Apology accepted. So does it?"

"The View? Yeah."

I leaned my head back and closed my eyes. I let out a small groan. "Great. A strip club. You couldn't just get killed in the parking lot, or an alley, like everyone else."

"I don't need this," she said, and turned to walk out.

"I really don't either, but it looks like we're stuck together."

She kept walking and I sighed as an unexpected sense of duty tugged at my mind. "All right, I'm sorry, come back. Besides, where would you go?"

She stopped but didn't turn around as she said, "I'd find someone else who could help me." Positioned like that, I got to see her nice, well-toned ass.

I stood in an attempt to wake up some and to stop staring at the dead woman's butt. I wasn't that desperate yet.

"I doubt it. As far as I know, or care, I'm the best there is in this town. Even if there was someone else, they'd never go with you to a strip club to check things out."

She turned around. "Why not? Are you guys all gay?"

"No. No we're not. Well, aside from San Francisco's Queen. But the point is neither are most ghosts. If you can see what I can see, strip clubs are probably the most disturbing places in the world to go, next to hospitals. And they're even worse if you're a female ghost. Means you get to get groped by guys who make the Elephant Man look sexy."

Her eyes grew wide again, this time out of fear. "They can't…rape me or anything, can they?"

"As a matter of fact they can." I saw that she was about to cry again, so I quickly added, "Which is why you need to go as you looked a few minutes ago. That should keep most of them back."

"What about the ones it doesn't?"

I smiled. "I'll take care of them."

"Okay, and how am I supposed to get there? I'll just fall through the car."

"No, you won't," I said as I walked over to the closet to get my coat back out. "Old habits, like riding in cars and walking on the ground, die hard."

I took out my coat. "Now, if the question-and-answer session has come to an end, I'd like to get this nastiness over with as soon as possible."

*      *      *      *

The Nice View was a squattish, white building that had the sense of humor to be just half a block away from a Christian Life Center. You could wave to one from the parking lot of the other. A few cars occupied the View's sodium-lit parking lot, along with one battered and rusted van that the dead girl told me acted as the mobile closet for one of the more popular strippers. For reasons I could only guess at, the dead girl didn't point out her own car. Aside from the security guard and the milling throng of dead men, the parking lot was unoccupied.

"Why are there so many of them here?" the girl asked, staring out of her window.

"Well, think about it: you're a straight guy and you can suddenly go wherever you want without anyone seeing you're there. You're not going to hang about someplace boring like a graveyard or your old house or a hospital. You're going to go the strip club or the women's locker room. Which is why we need something to keep them out of our way."

Before leaving home, I'd remembered to reprovision my trench coat with a few knick-knacks that I figured would come in handy. Naturally, this included my favorite form of ghost repellent. I pulled a fresh cigar, nearly the size of a toilet paper tube, from a pocket and lit it after several attempts. Greenish smoke that looked more like a special effect from a particularly bad episode of The Twilight Zone than anything meant to be inhaled came rolling out as I blew air through it.

She wrinkled her nose and cringed back from the stench that suddenly filled the car. "How can you smoke something that smells like that? Is there a dead rat wrapped in the leaves?"

I opened my door through a man in a blue hospital gown. The ghost turned to me and was about to tell me to watch what I was doing, but he caught a whiff of the cigar's smoke and quickly backed away.

"I don't smoke it. I'd probably die if I inhaled one of these things. But they're great for wading through a crowd of horny dead guys. Vampires, too, actually." I studied the cigar for a moment. "Never thought about the rat thing. Guess it's possible."

"Are they even legal?"

23

"Not in the U. S. Now, put on your game face." I got out of the Sunbird and waited until the girl stepped through the passenger door to shut mine. A pair of ghosts that were walking toward me, one blue from asphyxiation, the other red from who knows what, immediately changed direction when I waved the cigar in their vicinity.

The girl, back to her former broken-necked self, met me at the back of the car. "Do your best to ignore the smell. Stick close to me and you'll be fine."

We made our way through the mass of dead men, with me blowing the occasional cloud of smoke out in front of us to act as a bulldozer to get any ghosts out of our way. A few got brave, but a faceful of a smell that'd make a septic tank seem fragrant was always able to convince them to back off. Pretty soon, we reached the mirrored doors. The security guard, who I could only distinguish from the dead by his lack of any fatal disfigurements, seemed unable to take his eyes off of me and the cloud of foulness that preceded us.

I held up the cigar to the man. "Want one?"

"No thanks," he said through clenched teeth as he fought bravely not to throw up. "I'm fine."

"Suit yourself," I said with a shrug. I opened a door with my free hand, just in time to be blasted by the opening chords of "Dr. Feelgood."

"Jainey's on!" the dead woman squealed, losing herself and reverting to her natural, stripper ensemble. She ran inside, pushing her way through a few ghosts with surprising ease.

I sighed and looked at the security guard. "Dead people. They never do what you tell 'em to."

I went in before he could come up with a reply.

"Did you pick that outfit out, or do they make you wear it?" I asked the tall man in a coatless tuxedo behind the counter. The yellow sweat stains blossoming from his armpits, along with a thin mustache that most thirteen-year-olds could outgrow, served to give customers a hint of the level of seediness they could expect from their evening.

"They make us wear them," he said like some sort of mantra he'd picked up with the payroll form for his job. "Why do you people always ask that?"

"Just trying to be conversational." I blew some smoke at him. Most of it dropped to the counter and slunk off into the shadows to suffocate dust bunnies, but enough made it to him to have its desired effect.

He backed up a step. "Whatever. It's twelve dollars."

I paid him. "So how's business?" More smoke threatened the man's lungs.

The cashier backed up some more and, seeing that the man with the nasty cigar wasn't going to leave until he answered the question, said, "It's bad. Now can you please take that awful cigar of yours and go watch the naked women?"

"Sure. Is...," I stopped as I realized that I didn't know my client's name. I made a mental note to try and keep my callousness a little more selective in the future.

"Is the cute girl in red leather working tonight?" I put my hand up to eye level. "She's about this tall, blond hair, goes about to her shoulders."

"You just described about a quarter of the women working here, man." The cashier motioned with his thumb toward the main area. "Why don't you go in and look for yourself."

I turned and started walking away, but I stopped before I got too far. A horrible thought crossed my mind.

"Is Andrea working tonight?" I asked over my shoulder.

"I think so," the cashier said quickly, hoping to get me and my cigar away from him as soon as possible.

"Dammit," I muttered and stalked into the main room. "I hate this job."

I grabbed a Styrofoam cup of coffee from Gimp Suit, the bartender, his eyes wide and pleading from the only open zippers in his leather cage.

"Sorry, nothing I can do to help you," I told the man in the suit. "Shouldn't have broken the deal."

The Nice View had a rather unique way of dealing with designated drivers who reneged and drank. Somehow, somewhere, someone with a particularly nasty sense of humor had cursed a black leather gimp suit so that it would envelope and possess whoever broke a deal with the suit. In this case, free non-alcoholic drinks for a designated driver as long as they didn't drink liquor. The minute they did, the suit would come after them. They'd be trapped in it, forced to give it a body, forced to tend bar for the Nice View, and forced to see every stripper who paraded across the stage but unable to do anything about it until someone else broke the deal and took their place. Luckily, though, this being a college town, they were usually only stuck in the thing for a day or two before they were replaced.

I looked over the crowd as I downed my coffee, the burning and the bitter, wet cat taste waking me up some. The living Tuesday crowd at the View was small. A pair of old men that I took as professors of some sort by their tweed jackets sat at a table close to the View's only stage and just left of the central aisle. Four migrant workers leaned on the stage, enjoying a stripper who was down to just her white, lacy panties, her artificially round breasts like mini beach balls just out of their reach. One of the workers occasionally brought his cup of pop under the counter and surreptitiously poured some liquor into it from a small, banged-up silver flask. The manager saw this but pretended not to, the large roll of ones sitting in front of the day-laborers convincing him not to. A kid with dreadlocks and a goatee, who I put at no more than twenty-one, was sitting back in a corner, watching the show by himself.

The living-impaired crowd was everywhere: on the stage dancing with the stripper, beside the stage, sitting in the chairs, on the tables, on the counter, and anywhere else they could fit. A few spectral women were there enjoying the show, too, sitting in a small group not too far from the stage. The more intimidatingly butch ones sat toward the edge of it, keeping men at a respectable distance with the occasional glare.

I shook my head at my continued run of bad luck.

I put the empty cup on the bar and made my way to my client, currently stuck just past the doorway because of the mob of the dead. They parted as soon as my cigar's stench oozed its way to them.

"You've got to stay near me," I told her through the din of Vince Neil singing about drugs and their dangers. "I can't protect you if you wander off."

I surveyed the candidates, both living and dead, for conversation prospects, and, as big of a pain in my ass as they tended to be, decided to go with the group of lesbians. They seemed the least driven by the habit of hormones. And I was pretty sure that I recognized one of them.

When we started toward the group, the stripper's ghost swept her hand through my shoulder, just missing my heart, in an attempt to stop me. "Wait! We aren't going to talk to ... them are we?" She looked wide-eyed at the group of women.

I suppressed a shiver from the coldness of her hand passing through me and looked at her. "First off, what's your name?"

She moved back a half-step, sensing something bad coming. "April," she said, her voice meek.

"Good. Well, April, don't put your icy little hand through my body

26

again. I'm not in the mood to risk a heart attack tonight, especially not for a karma job." Heart attack was a bit of an exaggeration, but I was trying to make the point that a cold swipe through the chest wasn't the most comfortable thing in the world.

"A what?"

"A karma job. Pro bono work. A freebie. And any job that makes me come here better pay off damn high in the good karma department." I mumbled the last as I stalked off toward the women, waving dismissively at the confused looks of the two professors, who had turned to watch as I had my angry conversation with the air.

"And yes, we're going to talk to them. Get over it." I picked up an ashtray as I walked and put out the cigar. I deposited the stub, a little less than half of the cigar, in a side pocket of my coat and tossed the ashtray on another table, sending it through a heavy-set guy in a hospital gown.

The guy started to get off of the table and move for me, swearing along the way, but a ghost next to him put an arm in front of him. The man holding him back shook his head and said, "Don't. It's the Detective."

The heavy-set guy put his hands up and sat back down, murmuring apologies.

I didn't pay much attention to this, too focused on what I was doing.

When I got to my destination, all eyes were on me.

"Ladies," I said expansively, with the biggest smile I could manage to fake. "How are you this lovely evening?"

"We'll be a lot better when you leave, dick," a husky female voice said from the right side of the table. "Although we just saw your ex's stage act about ten minutes ago, so that's a plus."

I'd been consciously avoiding looking at that side of the table, wanting to let my "friend" get in whatever barb she wanted to first. Doing so usually made her more amiable to my questions.

I looked over now, still smiling. "Taylor. How's my favorite example of just how wrong the church is doing tonight?"

It'd long been a running joke among dead homosexuals that they'd finally gotten to show the world that homosexuality was a person's nature and not a choice, and there was no one to see. Except for me, of course, and no church was in the mood to listen to "a rude little man who claimed to talk to dead people," as a priest had once said to me.

"Better once you and your dead tart get out of here," she said. "Did hanging out with dead people finally get to you, Roger? Gone necro on us?"

There were a few laughs at the table.

Taylor liked to over-indulge in altering her appearance now that she was dead. The form she presented was petite, with long, blond hair, blue eyes, and moderately good looks. I knew how she'd really looked in life, having gotten curious one time after catching a glimpse of her in her "true" ghost form. Taylor hadn't been overly attractive. The best word to describe her would have been plain. She was thin in a bony sort of way, with stringy, dishwater blond hair that always looked dirty. Her wardrobe choice, at least in the three pictures of her I'd found, tended toward browns, like she wanted to blend into the background. Knowing this secret had helped me to coerce her into helping me a few times over the years. Letting her insult me a bit allowed her to save face.

"Jealous that she doesn't swing your way?"

"I'm sure if I toss her a few singles she would." There was a round of open laughter at the table. "Isn't that right, April?"

"Shut up, you nasty dyke!" April shouted at Taylor, moving toward her.

Two women who would have been able to beat me senseless had they been alive moved over to intercept her. April stopped as soon as they did.

"Teach your dead whore some manners, Roger, or she's going to get a beating that it'll take her decades to come back from," Taylor said

I motioned for April to move back. Reluctantly, she did. "The dead whore, April, is the reason I'm here, Taylor. I wanted to talk to you about her."

Taylor shrugged. "She's dead, she's a whore, what else do you need to know?"

I sighed. "I don't have time for this shit, Taylor. Over-compensate for a bad life some other time. I'm tired, working for free, and I'm in a gods damned strip club. You know how pissy that makes me."

"Ask a Blood Hound. I heard one of them saw part of what happened," she said dismissively. "Other than that, I can't help you. Any other asinine questions?"

I thought about asking if she was the husband or the wife in her relationships just to piss her off, but thought better of it. I really wasn't that big of an ass, and I knew I'd regret it later. Mainly due to the large group of angry, dead lesbians that would be haunting me for the weeks to come. "No, I think that just about fills my quota of abuse for this part of the evening. Thanks."

"Uh-oh, Rick's coming over," April said, looking to my right.

Taylor smirked. "That's what you get for arguing with yourself." The table laughed again.

I turned to face the approaching manager and suppressed a smile. The man obviously lived under the mistaken impression that size equals toughness, leading to a stiff-armed strut in imitation of a bodybuilder's walk. Unlike a bodybuilder, however, the manager only had mid-sized arms with undefined muscles and a beer belly that preceded him by several inches. The thinning mullet only added to my amusement. I put him at about $20.

"Is there a problem, buddy?" Rick attempted to growl, but his nasally voice made it sound more like hay fever.

"None at all." I put my left hand in my pants pocket. "Just talking to some dead people." I pulled out a twenty. "Mind if I continue?"

Rick looked at the money, then back at me. He grabbed the bill and tucked it away faster than my eyes could follow. "As long as you're quiet about it. Don't bother the other customers."

I smiled. "Wouldn't dream of it."

Then, just as Rick was turning to leave, "Nasty what happened to April. Heard there was blood all over." Not that I knew about any blood at the scene, of course. It was just a good thing to tack on to a murder. He'd either correct me if I was wrong or go along with it if I was right.

Rick stopped and turned back. "It happens sometimes with strippers once the looks start going."

"You bastard!" April shouted. "My looks weren't going!"

She took a swipe at Rick and he shuddered in the middle of saying, "We'll get another."

"How sensitive of you," I said with no humor.

"Piss off, nut job." He turned, and this time I let him walk away.

Over my shoulder, I said, "She's feisty, Taylor. Too bad she's straight."

April looked like she wanted to hit me, but she held back.

"Good move," I said as I headed away from the table.

"Where are we going now?" April asked, joining me.

"The bathroom. We have to talk to whatever Blood Hounds happen to be here."

"We're going to talk to dogs?" She seemed less than convinced that I was serious.

"I wish. Dogs are at least sane, and if they aren't you can shoot them. The Blood Hounds are a group of ghosts that like the smell of blood. The worst ones get off on death and the smells that the body gives off during it. I have to shoo 'em away from my apartment occasionally." I shook my head. "This is just pushing all of my buttons. Thanks for a fun evening."

"It's not fun for me, either," April pouted. "You think I like being dead?"

"You're going to have to pretend to in a minute. The Blood Hounds like to hang out in the women's rest room, so you'll need to get one of them to come out to talk to me."

"Why do they hang out in the…oh."

"Yeah, and they like the dressing room, too. And not for the naked bodies."

April shivered as the thought of what had been secretly watching, and smelling, her fully hit her. "I think I'm going to throw up."

"You're dead," I said as we turned the corner and went down the four stairs to the bathrooms. "It's just a habit. You don't have a body to throw up with."

Before I could brief April about what she needed to do, a male scream echoed out of the women's bathroom. Several dead men came rushing out, knocking April out of their way and nearly freezing me to death as they went through me. My hand went instinctively to my coat pocket to pull out the cigar. It froze there when the final ghost loped through the door.

April screamed.

Anything can become a ghost; it just needs sufficient cause to do so. There are stories everywhere of phantom dogs, tigers, and even the headless ghost chicken that killed Francis Bacon. They were really rare, but I'd even heard a story or two from people I trusted talking about phantom dinosaurs, mainly down in the Yucatan. Human ghosts are just more numerous because they tend to have more reason to stick around than an animal. But there were other things, around and gone long before people had even evolved past rat-like things scurrying on the ground.

What walked out of the door resembled a human if it'd been crossed with a komodo dragon. Rust colored scales covered the creature's body, except for the stomach, where the scales faded to tan. Large, black eyes were set on the sides of an elongated face reminiscent of a Gila monster. Each hand and foot had three digits ending in claws long enough to gut a person without much trouble. It towered a good three feet over my head. The thing shifted its gaze to me and said in a voice that didn't seem made to say it, "Detective."

The lizard-man speaking shook me out of staring at it. "A naga," I growled as I pulled out the cigar. A lighter materialized in my other hand and I began puffing.

The naga reacted almost immediately, swinging at me with its left hand. I fell back, just about literally as my feet hit the steps behind me, causing me to stumble. It tried to move forward to take another swipe at me but couldn't push past my cigar's smoke. Nagas always were especially sensitive to smells, even more than human ghosts.

"Soon, Detective," the naga rasped before leaping through the wall across from the bathroom door.

"What the hell was that?" April shouted, terrified.

I blew as much smoke as I could in the direction the naga had disappeared. "Bad news on a level that I hoped I wasn't going to be playing on tonight."

I'd hoped that whatever had visited Suzie and her friends was something else. Something slightly less homicidal. Admittedly, this included pretty much everything in existence, but still.

Screams started to filter back from the main area. I went into the men's room to avoid the onslaught of dead people that were sure to come stampeding out shortly. Predictably, there were no ghosts in there. April stayed close behind.

"All right," I said and winced.

I looked in one of the bathroom's mirrors. Three thin lines of blood ran down my right cheek.

"It hurt you," April marveled.

"I noticed."

"How did it hurt you?"

"Lots more practice at being dead than most ghosts." It'd been a few years since a ghost had managed to physically hurt me. Come to think of it, it'd been a naga that time, too. A couple of them had figured out how to use sympathetic magik and hospital waste to make people kill themselves. Nasty week.

"All right," I said again, this time in what I hoped was a nice tone, with subtle menace underlying it and perhaps a touch of very displeased. "I want all of the cards on the table. What the hell have you gotten me involved in?"

"Nothing!" she protested. "I was killed. I want to know who did it. I've never seen that...thing before."

31

"Did you do drugs? Prostitution? Gamble? Anything that might have gotten you involved in something illegal or odd?"

"No, nothing. I just danced."

"Nagas don't appear where people just dance, hon." I pointed my still lit cigar in the naga's general direction. A puff of smoke shook itself free, hovered in the air for a moment, then decided to float to the ground. "If one of those bastards is here, then there's something going on."

I took a drag from the cigar without thinking and started hacking. "And I don't want to be there when it goes down," I said through tears.

"What is a naga?" April asked. "Is it some sort of monster?" Her eyes darted back and forth several times. "Are there more of them? Is it going to eat me? Is it…"

I blew some smoke in her face and she backed up. "Stop it. All you need to know is that they're evil bastards who hate everything that's alive, especially humans. They've been dead for eons, and they've got all that built-up anger to vent. They usually do it by trying to end the world."

"They? Are there a lot of these things?"

I shook my head. "Gods no. Only a few of 'em are still around. Maybe fifty. The problem is they usually avoid this city like it was genital herpes, or dead flies, or whatever bothers big lizards, because all of the other supernatural shit that's usually hanging around hates them as much as they hate us. If they're here, we've got bigger problems than you being dead."

April put her hands on her hips. "Says who?"

"Says the guy who can help you."

April seemed to want to argue the point, but dropped her hands to her sides after she gave it some thought.

"On a cheery note, though, I think that your death and Godzilla showing up are probably connected, so I'm going to keep looking into what happened to you."

She brightened some.

I pointed at her with the cigar. "But if you're involved in this somehow, you're going to be spending a few years in a urinal cake in this restroom enjoying some golden showers." I then pointed to one of the urinals.

This made April wilt some more and made me feel slightly better. If I couldn't get back at the universe for messing with me on such a regular basis, I'd at least vent some of my frustrations on its latest attempt.

She started crying.

I began whistling "Piano Man" quietly in an attempt to ignore her.

"Wh-what are you whistling?" April said through sobs.

I stopped. Listening to Billy Joel was one of my guilty pleasures, one that I did not want getting around. "Nothing," I said, and started whistling "Dr. Feelgood."

"I know I've heard it before…"

"Can you stay in one mode for bit?" I said a little harsher than I'd intended. "First you're a sad dead girl, then you're an okay dead girl, then you're a sad dead girl again, and now you're a curious dead girl. Make up your mind."

"I hate you!" April shouted, then ran through the bathroom door.

"Yeah, well, maybe the naga'll eat you and I can go to sleep," I said under my breath without any real feeling.

After a moment, I sighed, opened the door, and left. I went up the stairs slowly and stopped at the top. "Enter Sandman" blasted from the speakers as I peeked around the corner. A woman dressed in suggestive black satin pajamas took the stage, but no ghosts, naga or human, were evident in the small amount of area I could see. Which didn't mean there weren't any. Ghosts were better than car keys at hiding, and I could just sense a knot of them in the changing room by the stage that probably hadn't heard the naga.

As stealthily as I could manage, I stepped out and walked to the main room, puffing out generous quantities of green smoke as I went. Once I got there, the only people I saw were the day-laborers, a diminishing roll of ones in front of them. I relaxed a bit.

I let some of the smoke clear from in front of me and then scanned the room more closely. In the left corner, sitting at a lap-dance couch next to the strippers' changing room, sat April, crying into her hands.

"Dammit," I said quietly. "I hate dead women. Dead men never get all weepy."

Putting my free hand in my coat pocket, I made my way over to April. Stubbing out the cigar on the way over crossed my mind, but I decided against it. We'd be talking pretty close to the changing room, and I wanted to be able to ward off any Blood Hounds that might hear us.

"Stop crying," I told her as softly as I could with Metallica pounding its way through my body.

"No," April said without looking up. "I'm tired of you bossing me around and being mean to me."

I looked to the changing room a little nervously. I wasn't terribly worried about the Blood Hounds, but their tendency to be unpredictable could be a slight problem. Besides, I wanted to take them by surprise, not vice-versa.

Swallowing my pride, and forcing down as much of the irritation I was currently feeling as I could, I admitted, "I might have been a little hard on you back there."

She kept crying.

"Gods dammit." I stopped and took a deep breath. "We need to get on with this show. Caffeine's only going to keep me awake and chipper for so long."

April finally looked up at me. "Then go. You can do this without me."

"Noo," I said slowly. "No I can't. This whole thing is mostly just to get you to move on. And me back into bed."

"What about the lizard-thing?"

I ran my fingers through my still wet hair, annoyed at where I saw this going. "Yeah, there is that."

"So, you need me to stick around for something besides your sleep."

"All right, all right. I get the point. I'll try to be nicer."

"Try?"

I narrowed my eyes and puffed out some smoke. "Don't press your luck."

"Gotcha."

April wiped her eyes and stood up. "So, what now?"

"Now you go in there and get one of them to say his first and last name." I pulled out a urinal cake. "Once I've got that, I'll take care of the rest."

"How do I do that?"

"I don't know. That's your job. But I strongly suggest that you get out of there immediately after he says it. They won't be too happy with what's going to happen."

"What're you going to do?"

I held up the urinal cake. "Give one lucky contestant a luxurious new home. Now get going before they decide they've had enough fun tonight."

April waited until the current stripper's routine was over so the music wouldn't drown out her conversation, then put on her dead face and slowly walked through the lavender curtain that separated the dressing room from the club.

"Who the hell are you?" came a young male voice.

The next voice was low, grating, and drew out each word an extra syllable or two. "Noo sscennt onn herr. Shhe iss dead. Ignorre herr."

I smiled. It was not the kind of smile that was contagious, bringing joy wherever it went and lightening spirits. This was the smile of a sadist in a room alone with a bag full of puppies for a full hour. The kind of smile that brought out other smiles as a defensive measure meant to hide the fact that someone has just wet themselves in fear of it.

I recognized the voice and knew the owner of it quite well. In fact, I'd been waiting a long time for a chance to put the voice's owner someplace uncomfortable for an amount of time that's usually only used by geologists.

"Oops, I'm sorry," came April's voice. It had the innocent tone of air-headedness that has gotten more than one man to think with the wrong head. "I didn't know you guys were in here."

"Get out of here you scentless little twat." An older man's voice. "We don't need your bland smelling pussy in here. There's barely enough of the live stuff for the rest of us to breathe."

"But...," she started sobbing, "all I wanted was to know what's going on. I just woke up here, and nobody can see me! So I came back here to talk to the other girls, and they still couldn't see me!"

"Aw, jeez, I'm sorry lady," said the older man. "I didn't mean to make you cry or nothin'. It's just..."

"Idiot. Sstop talkingg to herr."

"But, Bloodscent, she's that chick that..."

"I ssaid shut up, youu moron," Bloodscent shouted. "Shhee iss..."

But Bloodscent didn't get to finish his sentence. I said, "Floyd Aaron Kramer," and his voice cut off. The urinal cake's inscription glowed white briefly. It shook some.

"Ah ah, Floyd. You're not getting away from me this time."

Shouting erupted from at least three men after I said the name. April came running out, back in her pretty form, followed by four men who stopped in their tracks when they got a whiff of the putrid smoke I'd started puffing out.

They were fairly standard ghosts: pale, slightly blotchy, and wearing the suits they were buried in. Except for the one on the left end, a nasty piece of work with most of his left side gone, the skin and flesh torn away in ragged strips that left bloodied tatters. I'm not sure what could do that, and I don't think I want to know, to be honest.

"Come on, boys," I said, clenching my teeth on the cigar. "I already cleared out everyone else. I'm more than happy to finish the job."

If they didn't know that the naga was the one who had done the impossible and emptied out the View, I saw no reason to not take credit. Especially if it got them to back down without a fight.

The one on the left looked like he wanted to try me, but his more complete friend next to him held him back.

"It's the Detective. Just let it go." The voice told me that this was the older man who had called April a twat.

I smiled and decided to push it just a bit. "Listen to your friend, Righty, and go back to smelling lady's underwear."

The torn-up man made as if he was going to come after me, but the older man held him back again. Finally, Righty flipped me off and said, "Fuck you," before turning around with the others and hobbling back into the dressing room.

"Sweet Home Alabama" started up as a cowgirl in Daisy Dukes and a tied-off, red plaid shirt strode onto the stage in her boots. I turned and headed toward April, dancing her old routine by the main room's exit. An all-too-familiar female voice shouted, "Roger!" from behind me, bringing me to an abrupt halt before I could get out the door, though.

"Shit," I said aloud, but low enough that the music drowned it out.

"I thought you didn't like coming here. Or was that just a lie?"

I took the cigar out of my mouth and turned to face the voice's owner. Andrea hadn't changed much since leaving me a few months back. She still kept her long black hair pulled back in twin pony-tails, lending her already young appearance more of a school-girl look. She played up the image by dressing in a plaid short skirt reminiscent of a Catholic school outfit, which she wore without the top, letting her naturally perky breasts see, and be seen by, the world. I'd felt them enough times to be able to attest to their authenticity.

"Trust me, it's not because I want to be. I'm on a case," I said, trying to look her in the eyes as I spoke. As nonchalantly as I could, I slipped Floyd's new home into a pocket.

Andrea sighed and rolled her eyes. "A real one, or an imaginary one?"

Andrea had never believed in my "gift" of seeing ghosts. She'd always considered my supernatural cases excuses to be out until all hours, doing anything other than what I'd told her I was doing. This mistrust, along with the obscenity that was my apartment, eventually led to our break up.

"They're all real, hon. Don't know why you could never understand that."

"So who's your 'client'?" she asked with a condescending smile.

"Funny you should ask. She used to work here. Her stage name was April."

Andrea narrowed her eyes and slapped me hard enough that I felt something in my neck pop. "That's sick, and you're an ass for saying something like that." She crossed her arms, hiding her breasts, much to my disappointment.

"If you say so, but it's the truth," I said, rubbing my tingling cheek. "I came home and found her ghost hanging in my closet not too long ago. And since I'm such a nice guy, I decided to help her with her problem."

"Which is?"

"Find out who killed her so she can move on. And unfortunately, she died here. So here I am."

"What do you get out of it?" she asked.

"Nothing."

Andrea glared at me.

"Seriously. I get the knowledge of a job well done, and some sleep. The sleep being the main reason I'm doing this."

"Now I know you're lying. You never do charity work."

I ran my fingers through my hair as I thought of another way to approach this. "All right. If it helps, think of it this way: I'm investigating April's death because I know it hasn't been solved by the cops, and helping them might get me on their good side."

Andrea put her hands on her hips, letting me see her breasts once again. Grudgingly, she told me, "They're saying it was a suicide, but we all know better."

"Why's that?"

"She's been too happy lately," Andrea caught herself, realizing she'd spoken in the present tense. "I mean, she was."

I smiled, trying to be reassuring. "It's okay. It's normal. Why was she so happy?"

"She had some guy she was seeing." Andrea looked around the room. "I thought I saw him in here earlier, but I guess not."

"What did he look like?"

"He's a young guy, kind of cute. Nothing special, really, but she liked him."

"Does he have a name?"

"Chip, I think."

"Did you get a last name?"

"Yeah, it was something real common. Jones. That was it."

That was more than I'd expected. When dealing with supernatural matters, names didn't usually just fall into my lap because names are power, as Floyd now knew. Except for the names of gods. Damned things did everything but mail out circulars.

"Was there anything weird about how she died?" I asked.

"There was blood all over the place, even though she'd been hung."

Which indicated a ritual of some sort. The kind of blood would tell me more about who or what it was for. Which meant more running around, unless Floyd knew something about it.

I decided I'd probably exhausted all of the questions she could, or would, answer, so I said, "Thanks, hon. So far you've been the highlight of my evening."

Andrea crossed her arms again. "I'm not sleeping with you, Roger, so don't think being nice to me is going to get me in bed."

"Damn," I swore half-heartedly. "Can't blame a guy for trying. Guess I'll just leave, then. Have a good night, Andrea."

"Is April really here?" she asked me as I turned to leave.

"Actually, she's over by the DJ booth," I said over my shoulder. "But yeah, she's here."

"Tell her…tell her I'm sorry," she said, but quickly added, "If she's really there."

"I will. It was good seeing you again. And thanks for not asking about the urinal cake or the cigar."

"One of the things I learned when I was with you was to not ask about things like that. Take care, Roger."

I walked over to April. "Let's go."

"How do you know Andrea?" April asked as we headed toward the entrance.

"Ex-girlfriend. She says she's sorry about what happened, by the way."

"That's sweet of her."

"Oddly enough, yeah it is."

We stopped when we got outside. News of the naga must've spread because the parking lot was empty. I started laughing, almost enjoying myself, and earned a glare from the security guard.

"What's so funny?" April asked me.

I turned my laughing down to a light chuckle and removed the urinal cake from my pocket. "'Bloodscent' here."

The urinal cake shook violently, but I managed to hold onto it.

April hugged herself, shivering a little. "You wouldn't laugh if you'd seen that guy. He was freaky looking."

"Oh, I bet he was. Floyd always had a pretty macabre twist to his imagination. Isn't that right, Floyd?"

The urinal cake stopped shaking, as if it was sulking.

"See, Floyd here and I go back a little bit. I once caught him watching my girlfriend, the one before Andrea, and me having sex. Seems he'd followed me back to her place from the View after I'd been there working a case. He decided to stay and was getting off on the smell."

April wrinkled her nose. "That's so...eww."

"Yeah, I thought so, too. I couldn't do much, though, until I found out his name. And by then he'd disappeared from the local scene, so I couldn't do anything." I held the urinal cake up. "Until tonight."

"So something good has happened because of me," April said.

I looked at her sharply, then finally smiled after a few moments. "I guess so. But it's not nearly enough to make up for all of the shit I'm betting is going to happen before we figure out what happened to you."

We started walking to the Sunbird.

"Can he talk in there?" April asked.

"No. I'll have to whip out the Ouija board to get any answers out of him."

April started to ask something but caught herself. Instead she just said, "Whatever works, I guess."

I grinned. "Now you're getting it."

*      *      *      *

I'd cleared off the remains of something from my coffee table and set a taped- and glued-together Ouija board on it. Sitting on edge, so it could roll wherever it wanted, was Floyd's urinal cake. It remained perfectly still as Floyd sulked.

"Why don't you get a new board?" asked April from next to me on the couch.

"Sentimental value," I replied absently.[3]

Then, to Floyd, "Listen up, Floyd. Unless you want to spend the rest of eternity locked in a safe-deposit box with a dead fish, you'd better help us."

Floyd rolled around the board, spelling out, "F-U-Q."

"I don't get it," April said, trying to figure the word out.

"Sound it out." I picked up Floyd. "I'm going to convince our fresh-smelling friend to help us. I'll be right back."

I left for the bathroom, leaving April still trying to guess what Floyd had spelled.

A few minutes later, I came back, smiling, with the dripping urinal cake. April was sitting with her arms crossed, an annoyed look on her face.

"I figured out what he spelled," she pouted.

"Good for you. There are cookies in the kitchen. Meanwhile, I just had one of the most satisfying experiences I've had in recent memory."

I put Floyd back on the Ouija board and sat down.

April looked at the urinal cake, wrinkling her nose. "You washed it off, didn't you?"

"You think I'm going to carry around something soaked in urine if I don't have to?"

"Just checking."

"So, Floyd, are you ready to help yet?" I asked.

Floyd rolled to the 'NO' space, leaving a trail of water behind himself.

I shook my head. "Floyd, I know you don't enjoy these particular smells, and I can keep going. I had a big bowl of chili earlier today that still isn't sitting well, not to mention whatever's hiding in my apartment. Now, help us and I'll just toss you in the nearest men's room. The binding will wear off after awhile. Or don't, and I'll set you downwind of the paper mill after I've had my fun tonight, and we'll try again later."

Floyd rocked back and forth as if deciding. Finally, he rolled slowly over to "YES."

[3] My "gift" first manifested when I was thirteen. My friend Jacob Dane and I were using this Ouija board to ask typical thirteen-year-old questions (Will I be famous? Will I be rich? Will I ever get laid?), when a third pair of hands, this one considerably larger, greyer, and deader, were placed on the pointer. I did a slow pan up to the smiling, rotted remains of an old woman's face, nearly wet myself, and ran out of the room. I went back there years later, when I first became Kalamazoo's Detective, and helped the old woman move on. Turned out she just needed to tell her son she was sorry. Never knew what for. Not really my place to ask. Jacob had left the board there, so I asked his parents if I could have it.

"Good boy, Floyd. I knew we could count on you."

I leaned forward. "Now, first off, do you know who killed my client here?"

Floyd stayed on "YES."

"Who?"

Floyd spelled out, "N-A-G-A-S."

I sat back. "Damn. It's times like these I wish I believed in gods."

"But they're just ghosts," April said slowly, trying to see if there was anything she wasn't getting. "How can they hurt people?"

"Possession," I told her. "They take over someone's body and make them do what they want. It's hard to do, though, unless the person is willing. And I can't think of anybody dumb enough to let a naga rent their body for an evening of stripper murdering."

There were a few other nasty possibilities that I really didn't like considering. Like taking over a person's body completely by evicting his soul. Eviction was the permanent form of possession. It took a lot to do since there are few things stronger in the universe than a soul's link to its body, but it wasn't impossible. Especially if there were several nagas working together.

Another unsettling option was that they'd squatted in a dead body. One of the worst things I'd ever seen was a dead body occupied by a ghost that just refused to give up the flesh. He had to keep it fresh by eating living tissue almost constantly. Preferably human. The apartment he was living in, and I use the term "living" in its loosest form, made an abattoir seem like a perfumery. Rotting scraps of meat and organs lay scattered throughout the place, attracting rats and bugs, putrefying in sickening waves of summer heat and stench. And the body itself looked like a man-shaped leather sack full of squirming puppies trying to nuzzle their way out. I think I took sleeping pills for a month after that one.

"Who was it, Floyd?" I asked the urinal cake. "Who's our naga riding around in?"

Floyd spelled out, "D-O-N-T (pause) K-N-O-W."

"Bullshit. You were probably there watching and smelling it all."

Floyd rolled over to "NO" and then spelled out, "G-O-T (pause) H-E-R-E (pause) T-O-D-A-Y (pause) H-E-A-R-D (pause) S-T-O-R-Y."

"Who from?"

"J-I-M-M-Y."

"That lying piece of dead trash? I wouldn't trust Jimmy as far as I could toss the car he's in. I thought you were smarter than that, Floyd. You'll have to do better than him as your source."

"The car he's in?" April asked.

"Pissed off the wrong people. Got put in a trunk and turned into a cube of metal," I said. "Stay focused."

To Floyd I said, "What about it? Have any better proof?"

Floyd rolled over to "NO."

"Damn."

Picking up on my frustration, April asked, "What do we do now?"

I sighed. "Now we go see Beth and Mama Rosa. And if they tell me there are gods involved in this mess, I'm going to be seriously pissed."

"I thought you didn't believe in gods."

"I don't. It just encourages them. But that doesn't mean they don't exist."

"So there's someone up there looking after us?"

"Nope. It's just us. Sometimes they help out, but only if it's in their best interest. Usually they just cause trouble." I got up, saying to myself as I walked away, "Bastards have almost blown up the world more times than I can count."

Before I got five feet from the couch, though, I turned, walked back to the coffee table, and picked up Floyd. "You're coming too. Don't need you rolling off somewhere I don't want you."

I put Floyd in a trench coat pocket before I put it on.

"All right, let's go see Mama Rosa."

April stood up. "Will she be up this late?"

I laughed with no real humor. "She's a reincarnated fortune-teller. She's probably expecting us."

## 3.

The rain was coming down in full force.

"Is it just me, or does it look like someone's just dumping buckets of water on us?" April marveled as we pulled to a stop in front of Beth's house.

I glared at her. About halfway there, I'd realized that I'd forgotten an umbrella. "Says the woman that rain just passes through."

I looked at the house. Light could be seen glowing behind a shade that blocked out the large picture window.

"Really going to be pissed if some god's in on this," I mumbled again.

I got out of the Sunbird and dashed to the door, swearing the whole way. It was already opening as I reached it, so I just darted inside, overshooting the doormat and sliding another foot across the well waxed floor when I tried to stop. I flung out my arms and managed to steady myself before my feet went out from under me.

"That was graceful," Beth said from behind me.

"Screw you, Beth," I said, turning to face her. "It's late, I haven't gotten any sleep, I had to go to the View, and my caffeine buzz is wearing off. I'm not in the mood."

"Then go home, get some sleep, and come back in the morning if you're going to act like that," Beth said, meaning every word. "I don't care if the world is ending. You're not going to talk to me like that."

I ran my fingers through my hair to get some of the water out of it. "Sorry. It's just been a rough day."

"That's better."

"Nice outfit, by the way," I said, referring to the pink and white cotton nightgown she was wearing.

Beth had everything I looked for in a woman and more. Her hair was long, thick, and red. Her face and body were not quite beautiful but that half-step away from it that made her seem attainable. The kind of beauty that flaws only accented. She was also very well aware of what went on in the city. Probably, and I'd never admit this to her, more so than me. Her knowledge of the city's supernatural events had gotten me, and Kalamazoo, out of more than one debacle.

The "and more" part, though, was one of the reasons she and I had never actually gotten together as anything more than associates. The "and more" consisted of Mama Rosa.

Beth looked down and ran her hands over herself. "What's wrong with my nightgown?"

I smiled lasciviously. "Nothing. I just wanted to see you touch yourself like that."

She came over to me and smacked me hard in the face, smiling. "Ass," she said gently.

I winced. "Watch the face. I had a little too close of an encounter with a naga earlier. And Andrea. You wouldn't think it, but that woman's got an arm on her."

April walked through the door just as Beth did this. "Is there anybody you're not a bastard to?"

I looked at her, rubbing my face. "Not as far as you know."

"He's especially rude to women he thinks are cute."

"She can see me?" April asked.

"No, to both comments," I said. "Beth's just mad that I won't go out with her because of the old lady living in her head."

"And I'm just used to him coming over with invisible friends."

"Better than listening to voices in my head," I replied.

April looked at Beth. "Is she crazy?"

"That was funny the first twenty times," Beth said to me. "Can't you think of anything new?"

"You've got an eighty-year-old woman in there with you," I said back to her. "Nothing is new to you."

Beth's smile grew at this. "It's good to see you, Roger. Now, take your coat off," she said softly. "We've got a lot to talk about. I'll go get the tea."

"Dammit." Tea meant it was serious.

Beth went into the kitchen. I took my coat off and set it on the floor next to the door so the water that had soaked through it could puddle off someplace easily cleanable. The living room was a decent size and still smelled of new furniture. She'd had to replace all of the old stuff after the Fimbulwinter incident. The Fenrir wolf had managed to find its way into her house and destroy almost everything in the living room. The large blue area rug covering the majority of the wooden floor served mostly to hide the claw marks it'd gouged. She'd fit two couches, one blue and one vaguely beige with prints of water mill scenes all over it, on opposite walls. A matching blue chair sat next to the blue couch and across from a large, heavily locked oak trunk that always felt like it was looking at me with more than a little disapproval. A semi-circle coffee table occupied the center of all of the furniture. I sat in the chair.

April looked around the room. "Where should I sit?"

I began flexing my fingers to get out some of the stiffness the cold rain had put in them. "The blue couch. Mama Rosa likes to be on the other side of the table."

April walked over to the couch and sat. "So what's her deal? And why do you keep calling her Beth and Mama Rosa? I mean, which one is she?"

"Both. Mama Rosa died about a hundred years ago and came back as Beth. Beth began to remember her past life about ten years ago, and Mama Rosa came with the memories. She's basically a thirty-year-old woman with an eighty-year-old woman in her head. And together they're the only real fortune-tellers in the tri-state area outside of a few gods, the Fountain, and the Water Street Oracle. If there's something big and horrible going on, she'll know about it."

April stood up. "Then why didn't we go to her first?" She gestured harshly toward the kitchen. The seriousness of the motion was completely destroyed because it caused her breasts to jiggle wonderfully. "Why'd we go to the View and go through all of that other crap if we could've just come here?"

"Cause, darling, he couldn't," came an old, scratchy voice from the kitchen's doorway. "Roger knows better'n to come bugging Mama Rosa 'bout every little thing. It just wouldn't do."

I looked over and saw Beth carrying a tray with two cups and a teapot. She was hunched slightly and looked somehow smaller. Her face had become sagged and wrinkled. Mama Rosa shuffled slowly into the room and set the tray on the empty coffee-table.

45

"Evening, Mama Rosa," I said to her as she carefully sat down, as if the rain was bothering her arthritis. "How've you been?"

"Oh, can't complain none," Mama Rosa poured a cup of tea. "Don't mean I stay quiet, though," she finished, smiling, and filled the other cup.

I looked to April. "And before you ask, yes she can see you, and no I don't know how she can and Beth can't."

"Beth was right," Mama Rosa said as she picked up her cup. "She is a cute one."

I reached forward and picked up my cup. "And she's also a dead stripper. Cute just isn't enough for a relationship in this instance."

"That is a problem."

Mama Rosa took a sip of her tea. "How'd she die?"

"Well, she appeared to me hanging, but Andrea said there was a lot of blood, so I'm not really sure yet." I sipped my tea. "I'm leaning toward hanging, with the blood being from something else."

Mama Rosa nodded. "That sounds 'bout right."

"And the nagas are involved somehow. I thought you could help me with how and why."

"She was hung. Ain't no doubt 'bout that. Ghosts gotta show up how they was killed. You know that."

"Yeah, I do. I was just hoping that maybe it was more of a trend than a rule."

We both drank our tea in silence for a moment.

April couldn't take it anymore. "Whose blood was it? What's going on?"

I yawned and rubbed my eyes with my free hand. "Not whose, what's. Probably a chicken's blood. Looks like we've got some voodoo going on."

"No and yes, Roger," Mama Rosa said. "It's voodoo, but it wasn't chicken's blood. It was snake's."

I nearly threw my cup on the floor. "Damballa's here? I thought he couldn't come back for a hundred years after the shit he pulled in the War of Storms."

"Them naga's have been busy critters of late. They helped him get 'round the banishment."

"I really find it hard to believe that Damballa's stupid enough to deal with the nagas just for that. A hundred years is nothing for a god, especially one as old as Damballa."

"That's just it, hon. They are giving him something else, but we haven't heard what it is. And we don't know just what they're getting out of the deal."

"Dammit," I almost shouted. "That would explain Vesta's warning. I really didn't want to deal with any gods on this one. Especially voodoo gods. Now I've got to burn my hair and nail clippings and actually use something other than the smell to keep things out of my apartment. Have you called up Yomyael yet?"

"Beth tried, but he didn't pick up his phone. And that's another matter we're needing to talk 'bout."

"Who's he?" April asked.

"A former fallen angel that lives over in Portage who likes to study religion," I said. "He just about never leaves home, though. He's sort of become addicted to reality TV lately."

"He's a demon?"

I shook my head. "Yomyael was a Grigorian angel, the ones who fell in love with humans way back when and started having kids with them. God wasn't too happy about the whole situation, so he killed all of their kids and clipped the Grigorians' wings. God finally forgave them a year or so back, making him one of the few gods that could admit he was wrong if you gave him a few thousand years. You think Damballa got him?"

Mama Rosa ran a finger around the edge of her teacup and stared into its depths. After a few moments of this, she finally said, "No. I think on him and all I see is a weasel in the night."

"And for those of us who don't get prophetic visions that means...?"

"Revenge, sneaking up on him from a long time back. Something got him, all right, but it wasn't the old snake."

I sighed. "Then he's going to have to wait. I like Yomyael, but I can only deal with one disaster at a time."

"Is this Damballa guy really bad enough that you have to call up an angel?" April asked, a little worry creeping into her voice.

There were a lot of answers to that question. As far as gods went, Damballa was one of the quieter ones, only doing annoying or horrible things occasionally. He'd even helped me out some back when a nest of ghouls had decided to move into the big cemetery across from Kalamazoo College. He had some of the loas he controlled possess a few bodies and fight back against the ghouls, scaring them out of the area. However, he'd also killed Ishkur, the Mesopotamian god of storms, which was what had gotten him banished. And put him on my eternal shit list. Ishkur was never going to win the award for smartest god, but he was a hell of a guy, and I missed him. Saved me from Nergal once back in my early, stupid days.

I finally opted for, "Normally, no, but in this case, yes. He's sort of a snake god with roots back in Africa, so he's pretty old. Probably feels some weird connection to the nagas because of it. With the shot in the arm that voodoo gave him, he's pretty powerful, too. That and his sympathy for the nagas make him a potential problem for us."

I felt my heart jump. "And he usually hangs out with Baron Samedi."

The worry in April's voice was replaced with confusion. "Is he some guy from England?"

"He's the alcoholic voodoo god of death and dancing. Likes rum, smokes, and sex more than just about anything."

"Cept maybe causing trouble," Mama Rosa added. "And the bigger the trouble, the more he likes it."

Baron Samedi and I had a less antagonistic relationship than the ones I had with other gods. He was actually a fun guy, if you could get over his death aspect. Which was the reason we'd first met. A series of women were turning up dead who'd all gone home with the same guy the night before they'd died. They were young enough that natural causes didn't seem right, but nothing else pointed to murder. Turns out, Samedi had been seducing the customers and prostitutes of local gangbangers. And an unfortunate side effect of sex with him was death. As much as I wanted to be angry at him, he'd charmed me into seeing the harm the women had caused themselves and others, then took me out for a night of drinking. "Welcoming de new Detective," he said in his vaguely Caribbean accent.

"Luckily, Samedi's pretty easy to find," I said. "You just have to go to the place with the best rum in town."

"Too bad Ron don't like you none after last time," Mama Rosa said calmly.

"What'd you do?" April asked.

"Nothing you need to worry about. But yeah, Ron wasn't too pleased after my last visit to his place," I admitted. "Said he'd cut my head off and use my skull to hold his used condoms. Not that I blame him, I guess. What I did was pretty bad even by my standards."

"And you want to go visit this guy's place?" April asked.

"About as much as I wanted to go to the View, but I don't see another option."

"You know what you're gonna do if Baron Samedi's there, hon?"

Mama Rosa asked in a tone that said she was asking the question more out of habit than actual curiosity.

"Offer him some of that top-shelf rum you've got back in the kitchen."

Mama Rosa's looks hardened. "And what makes you think Mama Rosa's gonna just give you some of her tonic?"

"It might help stop the end of the world?" I tried.

"It's gonna take more than that, boy. Mama Rosa's seen forty ends of the world, not counting her end, and she's still here."

"Does the world almost end a lot?" April asked.

I shrugged. "It depends on the time of year. Winter seems to be the end-of-the-world season around here. This one started last month and doesn't look to be slowing down. Last season the end of the world nearly happened twice, but it almost happened four times the season before that."

I asked Mama Rosa, "What do you want for your 'tonic.'"

Her eyes gleamed. "A date."

Through some reserve of will that I didn't really think I had, I managed to keep a calm exterior while screaming in terror on the inside. "Won't Beth be kind of upset at you for using her body like that?"

Mama Rosa chuckled. "It's not for me, it's for her. It's mighty hard to meet the right kind of people doing this sort of thing. And I think you two are perfect for each other. And don't think I don't know what you're thinking, 'cause Beth's thinking the same thing. You wouldn't believe the names she's calling me in here."

April started laughing.

"I think I liked you better as sad dead girl," I said to her coldly.

April kept laughing. "Oh go for it. How many girls are actually going to go out with as big of an ass as you?"

It was Mama Rosa's turn to start laughing. "Too bad she's dead, hon. She's got spunk."

"Yeah, whatever," I grumbled as I stood up. "Just go get the damn rum. I'll do it."

Mama Rosa clapped her hands and got up. "Wonderful. Beth will bring it out to you. We'll be seeing you soon."

Mama Rosa's posture changed, going from her slightly slouched-over stance to Beth's fully upright stance. Her skin tightened on her face, then reddened. "Damn her! Why does she have to do that?"

"I think it's her weird way of showing how much she likes us," I said

49

more as a guess than an actual answer. I knew the old woman well enough to realize that she could've done it just because it amused her.

"Well, next time she can just get us a card," Beth said as she stormed into the kitchen.

There was the sound of a cabinet opening and then being slammed shut. A moment later, Beth returned with an unlabeled bottle of amber liquid. As she got closer with it, I could sense it like I did ghosts. Distilled spirits, made with the ghosts of sugar cane and gods knew what else.

She shoved the bottle at me. "Here. Now go save the world so we can get this nightmare over with." I took the warm bottle from her. "And if Damballa really is behind all of this, tell him I'm going to find him and bind his spirit in a garter snake and keep it in a terrarium for my next three lives."

I went over to my coat and picked it up, letting most of the water trickle off of it before putting it on. "Take a number. I'm going to put him in a plumbing snake and donate it to a local rest area to clean out their toilets."

April stood up and went over to me.

"Head out to the car," I said to her. "I'll be there in just a second."

When she'd left, for once not asking any annoying questions, I said to Beth, "You might want to go someplace safer than here. You're probably pretty high on their list of people to get to."

"No higher than you," she replied. "Be careful out there. Especially with Samedi. He acts like an idiot sometimes, but he's damn clever. If you give him half a chance, he'll kill you. Or worse."

"I know. Don't worry. I've gotten through stuff like this before, I'll do it this time, too."

I gave Beth a small smile. "Why is it that we can't be sociable to each other in front of other people, even dead ones?"

Beth returned the smile. "Just not in our natures, I guess. And it's hard to change your nature."

"I guess."

I opened the door. The rain had stopped. "I'll see you soon."

"You better. I don't want you dying owing me anything. Even some silly date."

After I stepped outside, Beth closed the door. I walked slowly to the Sunbird, where April was conspicuously waiting, and opened the door. She ghosted in. I set the rum in the backseat, started the car, and drove.

"Enjoy what you heard?" I finally asked.

She gave me a look of innocence that would make a newborn look like Charles Manson. "What do you mean?"

"I mean I know that you were listening in on us from outside," I said in a controlled tone. "I can sense where you are, in case you hadn't noticed. Part of my 'gift.'"

"You can sense me, but you couldn't sense the big lizard in the bathroom back at the View?"

"Too many ghosts to pick any one out. And don't change the subject."

"Okay, so what if I did? What's the big deal?"

"The big deal is that I need you to do exactly what I say when I tell you to do something. There are worse things out there than death, and I'm not real eager to experience any of them."

April crossed her arms and frowned. "You're just mad that I know you've got a girlfriend."

I gave her a look that caused her to sink down, literally, in her seat. "She's not my girlfriend, understand?"

"Whatever," April said quietly. "You love her."

"Which is why she's not my girlfriend. Girlfriends either get killed because of you, or get you killed."

April rose back up in her seat. "Beth's a big girl. I think she can take care of herself."

"I thought that about Erin, my girlfriend before Andrea, too," I said in a slightly subdued tone.

"Oh," April said, thinking she'd just made a huge mistake. "I'm sorry. I didn't know."

"Don't go getting all weepy on me again. She's not dead. Turns out I wish she was, but she isn't. She came close, though, when some dumb schmuck who'd got it into his head that he wanted to be the new Detective summoned a duke of Hell in her apartment complex's basement about four years ago."

I turned off of West Main and onto Solon. "Not that that's always a bad thing, but this jerk-off didn't know how to contain the thing, so it went on a small rampage. Luckily we had a date that night, so I was actually around to take care of it before it got too far. Plus the demon owed me one."

Aguares, a Grand Duke of Hell with thirty-one legions under him[4]. Someone with way too much imagination and not enough common sense had bound him in a beer stein to make it poisonous. I freed him. Nothing should be used like that, even a demon. Unless they've done something to deserve it, of course.

"If I hadn't been there, though, the complex, and probably that part of town, would've been a smoking crater."

The light on West Michigan Avenue and Solon turned red just as I got to it. "Now, unless you want to end up food or entertainment for something awful, you need to do exactly what I tell you. Especially when dealing with Baron Samedi. He's a god of death, so he can make you do whatever he wants unless you're ready for him."

"Can he hurt you, too?"

"Yeah, but he probably won't try to. He'll try to use you to hurt me." The light turned green and I drove.

"How? I can't really do anything to you."

"That you know of," I corrected. "Trust me, you can, and he'll know how to make you do it."

"So what do I do?"

"Stay in the car. I don't care if you think Jesus is out there telling you he's got free grape juice and fish sandwiches for everybody. I need you to stay here."

We drove on in silence until I turned off of Merril and on to Wheaton, one of the few remaining brick streets in Kalamazoo[5]. And with the Sunbird's shocks being less than outstanding, I could feel each and every one it passed over. A string of profanities broke the silence as every bump and jitter rattled every bone in my body then broke it again when I had to drive all the way up the street, turn around, and come back down because so many cars were parked along the road.

When we finally pulled up to the curb, April asked, "How many languages did you just swear in?"

"Eight, two of them dead. You pick up some pretty interesting stuff

---

[4] See what I mean about demon legions?

[5] Kalamazoo still has several, supposedly decorative, brick streets, the longest one over by Kalamazoo College. The real reason for them, though, is that the sound of cars driving over the brick lulls the horrors buried under them to sleep. Ecthru the Hunger sleeps under Wheaton's, dreaming of swallowing the world. Almost everything decorative in town is like that, from the Asylum Tower to the clock on South Burdick Street. Makes construction and demolition a nightmare.

doing this."

I got out of the Sunbird. "Remember: stay in the car."

"I will, I will. God, I'm not stupid."

I gave her a look that said I was unconvinced as I grabbed the bottle of rum and put it in my right pocket. I shut the door and began walking toward the house, only slipping once on the rain-slicked bricks.

A look to my left, down Davis Street as I passed it, brought out a shudder. Streetlamps lined the street, their orange light throwing everything into the kind of stark relief that you usually only saw in black and white movies. Or black and orange, in this case. Except for a few houses down, where even the light didn't seem brave, or stupid, enough to go. I'd seen it enough times in the daylight to remember what it looked like, though. A two-story house with chipped and faded blue paint squatted in that darkness. Broken chains dangling from the small porch's overhang moved lazily in the wind, perhaps in memory of the swing that had been there. Long-dead bushes, planted by the house's overly optimistic former owner, almost covered a gap under the porch just big enough to let in the occasional small child who didn't know better than to go exploring under it.

"And the Evil House is asleep tonight."

I kept walking. Ron's house was another old two-story that sat on the corner of Wheaton and Merrill. About a year earlier, he'd gotten ahold of me to come and take care of a ghost that was haunting the upstairs. A simple unfinished-business haunting, I was able to get it to move on pretty quick. After that, he'd started inviting me to his after-hours parties. Until the... we'll say "incident," anyway. I missed the parties, if just because of the drunk college girls and free liquor. His drink of choice, a brand of rum supposedly imported from a mission in Jamaica where resident monks made only three casks of it a year, was the reason Baron Samedi showed up so often.

A rosy glow emanated from the first floor window on the house's Wheaton side. A thick grey blanket covered its interior to help keep the sound of the music inside from reaching neighbors who might call the police. The porch was empty, which was odd. If the large line of cars along the roads indicated anything, the party was fairly packed, which always meant a few smokers hanging outside getting their nicotine fix.

I walked up the porch steps and opened the front door. Despite the chill in the wet air, a warmth began to tendril its way through my body starting at my groin, making me feel the cold loneliness outside all the more. I took my last breath of fresh air and went inside, slamming the door before too much of the loud, unintelligible music rattling my insides could escape.

"Ah, damn," I mumbled, mostly out of habit because nothing short of shouting at the top of my lungs could be heard at the moment.

I'd expected a good amount of drunk people, dancing, and general partying. They were normal for any party that picked up where the bars had left off and played host to a god like Samedi. I hadn't, however, expected to walk into a muggy house full of people dressed for the tropics. Which is to say either not dressed at all, or close enough to naked to make no difference.

Men and women groped, kissed, caressed, and sexed each other on the large staircase in front of me, on the floor of the living room to my left, on the couches, and pretty much on every flat, or at least semi-flat, surface they could find.

"The View and now this. When did my life become a porn movie?"

This copious amount of exposed flesh, a smell only the lizard part of my brain recognized, and the balmy temperature all made me want to take my trench-coat off and join in, find a willing partner, and just have a good time. It was like the heat, both atmospheric and physical, and the hard, heavy beat of the music were whispering to the animal part of my brain, telling me to enjoy myself. To forget what I was doing for a while and relax. I deserved it, after all. Perhaps sidle up to the trim blond who looked so lonely with only one partner.

I very nearly did, too, but that little bit of my mind that hated being told what to do prevented me just long enough to think about what was going on.

In spite of the sweat beginning to trickle down my back, I managed a smile. "You're not getting me that easily, Samedi."

I picked my way through the naked and semi-naked bodies, stopping occasionally to admire a particularly interesting or novel performance, then moving on. After threading my way through the sun room next to the living room, I made it to the kitchen. As I knew I would, I found Baron Samedi there, a bottle of rum in one hand, a perky woman a lovely shade of caramel in the other. A black walking stick with a silver skull on the top and a sharp, silver tip on the bottom leaned against the shelves behind him.

I always had to wonder what the average person saw in Baron Samedi. Goths and other assorted Mardi Gras types being attracted to him I could understand, but how an ordinary person could fail to be at least somewhat worried about a six-foot, two-inch, pale black man dressed in tails, a top-hat, no shoes or shirt, and carrying a black walking stick was beyond me.

At least the music wasn't as pounding in the kitchen.

"What is that piss-water you're drinking, Samedi?" I asked as good-naturedly as I could manage considering that large portions of my lower brain functions were seriously angry at not getting to join in the fun.

Samedi smiled hugely when he saw me, revealing more of his teeth than was humanly possible. "Roger me friend," he said in that odd Caribbean accent. "What in the name of Bondye's bones are you doing here?"

"Sweating my balls off because I know better than to take off even my coat when I'm around you."

Samedi laughed. "Don't be blaming me for your little problems." His eyes darted down to my crotch at the word little.

"Hey, I might not be a god, but I do all right."

"Den feel free to join in," the god said. "There's plenty to go around, even for someone as homely as you."

I shook my head. "Can't. Much as I'd like to, and believe me I would, I'm on the clock."

Samedi took a large swig from his bottle. "Suit yourself, but don't be coming here an' ruining tings de rest of us."

"Looks like you're almost out of rum," I observed.

"Dere's plenty more where dis one came from." Samedi winked. "Made sure of dat myself. Ron and me, we got ourselves an understanding 'bout the rum."

I looked to the woman Samedi had his arm around. "Would you mind letting us talk alone for awhile?" My cold, professional tone, combined with the amount of sweat currently dripping down my face, created an image that said this was not actually a question.

Samedi let her go and his formerly good-humored expression hardened, his skin pulling tighter to his skull and his eyes sinking into their sockets. "Why'd you go and do dat? She was going to be my entertainment for de night."

"She seemed like too nice a girl to wind up dead in the morning," I said flatly.

Samedi finished off his bottle. "Says you. I'll have you know dat she's a drug runner for her boyfriend. She's part of why half the people in dis area are hooked on crystal meth. Do you have any idea how many people have made offerings to me and mine to do something 'bout her?"

"We've had this conversation. That doesn't make her evil, and you know it. And she's in my town, so she's under my protection. Besides, I've got this to help make it up to you."

I pulled Mama Rosa's rum out of my pocket and Samedi's features returned to human. His eyes widened in delight and desire.

"Maybe I was wrong 'bout you, Roger. You're okay." Samedi reached for the bottle, and I put it back in my pocket.

"Not so fast."

Samedi's eyes sank away, leaving two black pits. "I'm thinking it's best if you don't do dat again, Detective. I don't take kindly to being teased."

"I'm not teasing. I'll give you the bottle as soon as you do two favors for me. The first of which is to come outside to talk. I think my ass cheeks are stuck together from this damned heat of yours."

Samedi's eyes returned as he thought my proposal over. "Fair enough."

I led the way to the kitchen door, opened it, and we went out onto a small porch. Samedi closed the door behind himself.

"What's the other ting you're wanting?"

I breathed in the cool air for a moment to clear my head.

"I want to know what the hell you and Damballa are up to with the nagas."

Samedi seemed surprised by this. "Is dat all?" He laughed. "An' here I thought it was something serious."

"Oh, you know me," I said conversationally. "I'm always making mountains out of molehills."

"'Specially here. All I did for dem was let one reincarnate as human a few years back in exchange for a bit of their belief."

I didn't see the point in this, but it still worried me. Nagas never did anything that wasn't planned out to their best interests. They weren't known to play well with others. And their hatred of humans made it even stranger that one would reincarnate as a human. "What about Damballa? What did he do?"

"I don't know, and I don't rightly care. What he does is his business. Now, give me de rum."

"Where's he at?"

"You said two tings. Dat would be three."

"Dammit," I said under my breath. I took out the rum and handed it to Samedi.

Samedi opened the bottle and smelled it. His eyes closed for a moment. "Dis is some good shit you've got here, Detective. It's old, and it's made of tings I'm betting you don't want to be knowing 'bout."

"You're probably right," I said, still thinking over what I'd just learned and the amateur mistake I'd made.

Samedi took a sip and held it in his mouth, savoring it before finally swallowing it. "Some day, when you owe me one, I'm gonna get you to tell me where you got dis. Humans shouldn't be having dis type of drink. Maybe I'll tell you where Damballa is for it?"

"I'll take your word on the rum. And I'd rather find Damballa myself. You can bet you'll never have one over on me."

"We'll see, Detective," he said, smiling. "We'll see."

"Are you sure that's all they wanted?" I asked, not wanting to let this subject die before I understood it better.

"Dat's all."

I shook my head. "I don't get it, but something about this is just bad."

I pulled my sweat-soaked shirt from my body. "And you should know better than to deal with them. You know what they do."

"It seemed harmless enough. Plus it got rid of one of de horrible tings, putting it in a human. Maybe we'll get lucky an' he'll end up in Hell when he dies."

"Maybe. I just don't see why you do this shit, Samedi. All of you gods. Even for a little belief. You know it's just going to end badly."

"I'm no god, Detective, I'm just-"

"A humble spirit in the service of Bondye. Yeah, I know. Tell it to someone who doesn't know about syncretism."

Samedi laughed. "Fair enough."

He thought on this for a moment. Finally, he just shrugged and said, "We're gods. It's what we do. Any little ting we can be doing to get some belief, we're gonna do it. Even if it's gonna cause de world to end. 'Specially if it's gonna do dat, 'cause de more spectacular de event, de more belief dere is. An' de more belief dere is, de more we are."

"Pretty sick," I said without much feeling. "One of these days, you're going to do something that people like me aren't going to be able to prevent, and the world really is going to end."

Samedi gave his inhuman smile again. "Never. I have faith in you folks. No matter how bad I screw up, you're always gonna be dere to stop it."

"I hope so. I'd hate to end up like the nagas."

I walked down the porch's steps, stopping at the bottom. "By the way, where's Ron? I didn't see him in there."

Samedi took another slow sip of his rum. When he was finished, he replied, "In his bedroom with two other gentlemen, having de time of his life I imagine."

I smiled, genuinely amused for possibly the first time that evening. "If I survive this, Ron and I are going to have a rather long conversation about inviting me to these parties again. Have a good night, Baron."

"And you, Detective. Good luck saving the world. Least make sure she lasts the night for me, eh?"

\*             \*             \*             \*

As I walked back to the Sunbird, I glanced toward the Evil House. April's ghostly form, back in its just-dead appearance, was making its way slowly down the sidewalk.

I dropped my head so that my chin hit my chest. "I should just let her get eaten by the Evil House."

I debated this for about five seconds, but finally decided it'd be bad for my reputation if one of my clients got herself eaten, no matter how much easier it'd make my night. I walked as quickly as my tiring body would allow, slowing down to keep pace when I reached her.

"I suppose you're in some sort of trance," I started, casually, "and can't resist going down to the horrible, soul-devouring house because you GOT OUT OF MY CAR."

Not that shouting at her did any actual good, but it did make me feel better.

I took out the remains of my rancid cigar and lit it. When it was good and fired up, I sucked in smoke until I couldn't hold in anymore. I dropped the cigar on the ground and covered my ears. Then I blew the smoke in her face.

April's previously dull eyes instantly turned red, and she changed back to her stripper body. She screamed loud enough that dogs for miles around began barking madly and a few babies woke up wailing.

When she finished, I removed my hands from my ears, stubbed the cigar out on the ground, and put it in a pocket. "Next time stay in the damned car," I said and turned around. I started walking back to the Sunbird.

"What was that?" April asked as she followed me, terrified without quite knowing why.

"It was just the Evil House trying to eat your soul. Think of it as a black hole for ghosts."

She walked faster. "What's it do?"

"Same thing any black hole does. It sucks things down into it forever. If you'd stayed in the car, this whole situation could've been avoided. And thanks for waking it up, by the way."

April looked over her should briefly. "How does a house wake up?"

I opened the Sunbird's driver's side door and got in, waiting for April to walk through hers before I closed mine.

"Normally it doesn't," I said, "but that one has something in it."

None of Kalamazoo's past Detectives had any idea just what the Evil House had in it, or why it acted the way it did. Or if they did, they hadn't written the information down anywhere that I'd found it. All any of us knew for sure was that it was evil, and that it thought ghosts were tasty. Admitting that you know nothing about something as big and scary as the Evil House is never a good move in my business, though.

I started the Sunbird. "Let's talk about this somewhere else."

We drove down Wheaton and I turned toward the Evil House. As we passed near Ron's house, I gave it a longing look. "I'm really starting to hate this job," I said quietly, shaking my head.

"Why's that?" April asked.

I just glared at her. A dull, throbbing ache began behind my eyes. I put it down to an aftereffect of Samedi's influence. Dumb, really, but I wasn't paying attention to where I was going.

"Right. Silly question."

"I would've said stupid."

April ignored this. "Where are we going now?" she asked as we headed toward Oakland Drive.

"We've got a few options, none of them all that good. There's the Fountain, who's close but a pain in the ass." I turned left onto Oakland Drive and the ache flared to a mild pain. "There's Papa Legba, if he hasn't gone south for the winter and you don't mind leasing out a decade or two of your afterlife to him. Or, if things are as bad as they sound, there's always Jakobar, if we can find him and his ghost has come back to warn him that he's going to die soon."

"What?"

"Long story involving time travel. I try not to think too hard about it."

The mild pain turned into a full-blown headache, causing me to actually look at where we were. We'd gotten near the Kalamazoo Psychiatric Hospital, giving me a clear view of Asylum Tower, pulsing out blue light into the orange sky like a nuclear power plant about to go critical.
I could only stare at it as rational thoughts fought their way through the pain and a not-small level of terror.

In theory, Asylum Tower was just a bricked-over water tower sitting dead center of the hospital. This didn't explain why the thing looked more like the last remnant of a castle than a water tower, though. You had to wait to see that. At night, if you had my ability to see ghosts, the thing lit up like an electric ice cream cone topped with crazy. The true purpose of Asylum Tower's design, and its placement on the highest point in the city a hundred years back, was to contain the spirits of the crazy people that had died in the city over the years. And there'd been a lot of crazy people. Enough that all I could normally make out was a haze of blue spiritual energy rather than individual ghosts. Their screams got through, though. Each and every one, tearing into my mind like sewing needles, scraping it away sliver by sliver. Normally all it gave me from this distance was a small ache in my sinuses that went away pretty fast. Of course, normally it didn't shine so bright that Martians could see it.

April followed my gaze. "Oh my God. What is that?"

"An omphalos for dead crazy folk. Worried, dead, crazy folk by the looks of it."

"What's an omphalos?"

"A center of the world," I said, pain bringing tears to my eyes. "Pins the sky to the earth, makes it kind of a neutral zone."

"Don't you mean the center?"

"No. Great thing about religion. You can believe all sorts of things that don't make sense. Including that the world has more than one center. Kalamazoo's got about a dozen of them."

I slowed down. With a great deal of effort, I pushed the waves of pain in my head back and watched the ebb and flow of energies pulsing around the Tower. "Something big is up. They're trying harder than usual to get away from the Tower."

"Should...should we help them?"

"Can't. Been trying for years to figure out how to get them to move on. Short of knocking down the Tower and letting them all out at once, they're stuck. Best we can do is find out what the nagas are doing that's got them all riled up. Hopefully that'll settle them down. Unless we get really lucky, and they're scared of something else…"

A car behind me honked. I flipped him off and sped up.

"All right," I started, annoyance tingeing my voice, "we're going to the Fountain. It might know what's going on."

"It's not something else that can eat me, is it?"

I sighed as the psychic pain began to let up the further we got away from the Tower.

"No. It's an oracle, of sorts. It's easier to just show you."

"Is it like a wishing well?" April said excitedly, thinking she had started catching on a bit more.

I thought on this. The Fountain was the occasional home to the spirit of the Kalamazoo River. The idea of it being anything like a wishing well was something like asking if a dolphin was like a shark. Yeah, they looked similar, and you might be able to play with both, but the games rarely ended the same. It and I had a long history that boiled down to seeing which of us could piss the other one off the most. Usually this involved it giving me just enough information and misdirection to nearly get killed, which pissed me off. My first taste of our future relationship happened a year after I got shanghaied into being Detective. I'd needed information about the Cult of Cleaver's latest attempt to bring about its fifties sitcom-inspired vision of paradise. After mooning me, the Fountain happily told me where they were hiding out. He neglected to inform me that they'd brought along a couple of earth elementals as bodyguards, though. My ribs ached for months after that beating. I always survived these encounters, no matter how devious it thought its lies had been, pissing it off. It'd only helped me once without openly trying to get me killed. In the War of Storms, Indra had tried to flood the region, which would have destroyed the Kalamazoo River as an individual, so it had needed me as much as I'd needed it. We'd both agreed to never discuss the temporary truce again.

"No. It doesn't grant wishes, it swears like a sailor, and lies as much as it tells you the truth about whatever you ask it."

"Sort of like you?" April said with a completely straight face.

I narrowed my eyes. "Never compare me to the Fountain. It's an evil bastard that gets its jollies by being rude to everything. I'm a fairly good bastard who just doesn't like people. There's a difference."

April rolled her eyes. "If you say so."

61

I yawned. My caffeine buzz was wearing off, and there was a distinct emptiness to my stomach. "Maybe we should go to Brew's Diner first so I can get some food and think everything over first."

"Oh God. What's at Brew's Diner?" She had that now all-too-common feeling of dread in her voice that everyone gets if they're around me long enough. Not that I blamed them.

"Coffee and food," I said, covering my mouth as another yawn made its way out. "If I'm going to keep at this, I need a little bit of both

"You mean there's nothing weird or scary there?"

"I never said that. But in case you've forgotten, Miss Dead U.S.A., you fall into the weird and scary category yourself."

April blushed a little and looked away. "It's hard to get used to it."

"I've noticed. People not used to being dead are about half of my business and my karma jobs."

"For what it's worth, I'm sorry about ruining your night."

"You should be. But don't worry about it too much. I was mad at first, now I'm just tired and grumpy. If you didn't show up, I'm sure Beth would've called and woken me up."

April looked to me. "So you don't hate me?" she asked, a touch of hope in her voice.

"No more than I hate the rest of the world."

**4.**

A greasy spoon founded back in the fifties, something had happened to Brew's Diner shortly after opening. What, exactly, was anyone's guess. My personal favorite theory was that it'd been knocked out of Area 51 during a botched alien invasion. Whatever had happened, it had set the diner loose from most of its moorings in this reality. To my knowledge, no one knew where the diner's physical location actually was nowadays, but its door opened up to everywhere. A small broom closet in Beijing and a cellar door in Perth were a couple of the dozen or so places I knew of you could get to from Brew's, but I'd heard rumors of dozens more, some not even on Earth. Folks with more letters after their name than were in my name had tried to tell me how this was possible without magiks of some sort, but I always tuned them out after the word "quantum" just on general principle.

The general public remained pretty well unaware of the diner's existence because you had to know where one of its doors was to find it. Even then it could still be tough because they tended to hide. Kalamazoo's entrance was a plain, brown door on the backside of a local big box store, for instance. The general manager of the store knew about Brew's and let people use the store's parking lot in exchange for the occasional free meal and coffee break in Fiji. He usually remembered to turn off the security camera pointed at the door, but more than one potential Brew's customer has been chased off and threatened with calls to the cops by store security.

I winced at the amount of light that hit me as we walked into the diner. Brew was a theoretical physicist who was way too fond of shiny things, and every surface he could cover in polished chrome had been. Brew's grasp of taste and what human beings actually enjoyed surrounding themselves with when dining were also theoretical. Chrome tables, chrome booths, chrome ceiling fans, and on and on. Even the spots where the windows had been before the accident were flat slabs of undecorated chrome. The only color in the place came from adultery red cushions on the vinyl booths and counter barstools and the shifting neon glow radiating from a classic jukebox stocked with records dated no later than 1959. Brew made up for an interior even the Last Spartan[6] thought a little harsh by hiring the best short order cook in the tri-state area, which was why I came in every chance I got. Best burgers around. Coffee, too.

The diner was surprisingly deserted; one overweight ghost standing in the grill and inhaling the smell of cooking burgers made up its entire clientele. The cook, a one-eyed mountain of a man named Hrothgar, either didn't see him or didn't care. Hrothgar wore his long silver hair tied back in a braided ponytail and adorned with various bits of leather and metal. He had on kitchen whites, and I use this term loosely since they looked like they'd had their last washing during the Nixon years. Aside from short-tempered, I never could figure out what Hrothgar was, exactly. The diner wasn't technically part of Kalamazoo, so my ability to pick out supernatural things was weaker, and asking him just seemed tacky. The two live waitresses on duty, both new hires I didn't recognize wearing the Brew's uniform of jeans and a pink T-shirt, were sitting in one of the booths discussing their current lack of boyfriends. I assumed the burgers were for them. Betty, the ghost of a waitress who'd died about twenty years back, but refused to let that get in the way of her job, sat with them. Both she and one of the flesh-and-blood waitresses, an older blond named Theresa, if her nametag could be believed, got up and came to the door when we entered.

"Go ahead and sit wherever you want to," Theresa said through a fairly convincing smile. Her slumped shoulders told me that her cheeriness was faked, but I appreciated the effort. I'd probably feel that way too if I had to work in eighteen time-zones simultaneously.

"How's it going, Roger?" Betty asked. Betty either had the best

---

[6] You'd be amazed how many people had figured out the trick to immortality, or at least not aging; the Last Spartan, Jakobar, Erik Lionclan, and a dozen others I could think of off the top of my head. To hear them talk about it, the Sunday crossword puzzle was harder to solve.

self-image in the world or hadn't figured out that she could change her appearance. And I just didn't have the heart to tell her that dead folks didn't need that much eyeliner or lipstick. Or that her permed, blond hair, an obvious dye-job with grey roots showing, could've been fixed with a thought.

"All right," I said to both waitresses.

We made our way to a booth that gave me a clear view of the door. I sat with my back against the wall, a small comfort when you deal with things that could walk through walls, but it still felt reassuring.

Theresa started to set down a laminated menu, but I waved her off. "I'll have black coffee and a burger with fries, medium well. Thanks"

"You got it."

"Where have you been?" Betty asked as soon as Theresa left. "And who's the looker? Hi, I'm Betty."

April took Betty's outstretched hand and shook it. "April."

"April! Such a pretty name. I had a great-aunt, no, a second cousin named April." She lowered her voice. "Big girl. Never said no to a meal. Died in a plane crash when she was only twenty, poor thing. Maybe she knew something the rest of us didn't."

"Maybe," I said, distracted by the emptiness. "No offense to your second cousin, Betty, but it's pretty dead in here. Has it been like this all night?"

People, and things decidedly not people, always came to Brew's to eat. Even during the War of the Storms and Fimbulwinter it'd been busy. It's always breakfast, lunch, or dinner somewhere, after all. Empty meant people avoiding the diner for some reason. And if several seriously pissed off storm gods fighting it out hadn't been reason enough, I didn't think I wanted to know what was.

Betty nodded. "No one's been in here for hours. If it keeps up like this, we're not going to make anything in tips. I'm okay, but Diane, that's Diane over there. Nice girl. Not real friendly, but she'll loosen up. Diane needs rent money, and Theresa –"

"Can you give us a moment, Betty?" I said, cutting her off before she got off on too big of a tangent. "I need to talk with my client."

"Oh, sure thing. I know how it is with you Detectives and your clients. Gotta move 'em along. I'll catch you before you go?"

"Sure."

"She seems nice," April said after Betty had gone back to sit with the living waitress who still hadn't gotten a table.

"She is, but she can be a little too chatty. Comes from being stuck in one place for twenty years."

"Why doesn't she leave?"

"She's bound to the diner. It happens sometimes when a person feels particularly attached to a place in life."

"Stuck at work forever? Ew. Sounds more like Hell to me."

"Well, strange as it sounds to folks like us, some people actually like their jobs."

Theresa brought my coffee over. "Here you are. Need anything else right now?"

"Could I get a water, please? Thanks."

Theresa wandered off.

"Why didn't we just go to the coffee shop down by Ron's?" April asked. "It's a lot closer than this place."

"Because Zevon's Warren is a coffee house, not a coffee shop, among many other reasons. I don't need coffees, I need coffee. And my cholesterol level was getting dangerously close to normal. Nothing they have is anywhere near greasy enough to fix that."

"So you want to die," she said in the tone of the health-conscious lecturing the artery-hardened heathen.

I shrugged. "Assuming that I survive tonight. Based on what I've heard, a Detective's life is about as long as Betty's cousin's was, so I try to get what I can out of it. For me, that includes greasy burgers."

"Is it really that bad?"

I sipped some of my coffee, enjoying its bitterness for a moment. "Sometimes. Usually it's just routine hauntings or infestations by some of the dumber supernatural critters. Damn basilisks breed like rabbits around here for some reason."

Every year, the first week of June, I have to drive around town with a recording of a rooster crowing to exterminate as many of the things as I can. In some neighborhoods the kids know me as the chicken man. My high school guidance counselor would be so proud.

"Every once in a while, though, some god, demigod, or primeval force starts feeling ignored or bored, so it gets the urge to draw some attention to itself."

"How about the nagas?"

"They're kind of a unique case. They show up occasionally, try to wipe out humanity because they're still angry about being dead, and then disappear. They never make deals with humans or human gods, though. They think we're less than them. Which is why this whole thing with them, Samedi, and Damballa has me worried so much. Reincarnating nagas is an entirely new situation, as far as I know."

Theresa set a glass of water down for me. "Anything else for you two?"

"No, this is good."

She started to walk away.

"Miss?" I asked.

Theresa stopped and turned her head to look at us. Unfortunately, her body didn't turn with the rest of her, meaning she either didn't have a spine, or she was something nasty pretending to be human. And given all the places Brew's occupied, that list was a long one.

"I let on that I saw the ghost girl, didn't I?" Theresa, or whoever she really was, asked.

"Yeah, you did." I slowly lowered a hand to one of my pockets. "Are we going to have a problem?"

"Are you against me stripping your flesh from your bones and crunching them down like rock candy?" Her head began to rise up on a long, pale neck.

"You're a rokuro-kubi?" I asked, actually a little surprised. "I'd heard Tokyo's Kami Court killed all of you off."

"Not all. Never all."

Rokuro-kubi were, I guess still are, a minor nuisance in East Asian communities. Just like people, you get your good and your bad rokuro-kubi. Thing is, bad people don't usually start ambushing humans and living off their flesh and life force. Luckily, aside from the whole infinitely stretchable neck thing and exceptionally sharp teeth, they aren't any more of a threat than an average person.

I dove out of the booth and onto the floor as her head darted toward me. Teeth snapped loudly on the space my throat had just occupied.

"Use the cigar!" April shouted.

"You be nice to her, Roger!" Betty yelled. "She's one of the best waitresses we've had here."

The living waitress screamed from under her table.

"Would all of you shut up," I said as I got to my feet. "Trying not to die here."

Theresa's head swung toward me, but I was already gone, on my way to the kitchen.

I clambered over the counter and managed to land on my feet on the other side.

"You can't meander back here, Roger," Hrothgar said through a grey beard that couldn't have been up to health code. My burger was sizzling away on the grill in front of him, my fries in the fryer to his right. A pair of stainless steel reach-in coolers sat behind him.

The ghost standing in the grill just looked at me dully, too engrossed in the smell of the cooking food to really care about what was going on.

"Didn't really have a choice," I said.

Hrothgar, about to flip my burger, finally saw the head snaking its way behind me.

"Tyr's balls, I telled Brew something were amiss with that one." He threw his spatula down. "Your application asked if you were a yokai, fae, or other non-specified, non-human being, clear as crystals, it did. He'll be hearing about this, missy. "

Hrothgar looked at me. "Watch your foods, Roger. I have to script this down for Brew to gander in the morning."

"I could use a little help here before you do that, if you don't mind," I said, never taking my eyes off of Theresa. She'd stopped moving toward me when Hrothgar spotted her, rightfully intimidated by his large frame. Sure, a lot of it was fat these days, but he still had enough muscle under there from his younger days to make most people think twice about starting anything when he was around.

He waved me off as he walked toward a hall on the opposite end of the kitchen. "You can hold a simple little yokai. And if not, Brew will final her services when he comes. Either way, the lying tart will be extracted from my kitchen."

"Thanks, Hrothgar. You're a pal."

Then, to Theresa, "You don't have to do this, you know."

"Aw, is the brave and good Detective going to redeem my poor, cursed soul?" she laughed, coming closer.

"No, I'm just trying to keep you talking," I said, finally seeing what I'd come into the kitchen for. When Hrothgar had left the grill, he'd revealed a small, white bucket half full of brackish liquid sitting on a cutting board next to the grill. Three knife handles stuck up out of the bucket.

I ran for it.

Theresa's head shot out in front of me just as I was about to reach the grill. "Knives to cut my head off with? I always heard you were more original than that."

"Can't beat the standards," I said. Then I grabbed her still-extended neck and pressed it down on the grill. "But I am open to new ideas."

She screamed as the smell of cooking flesh filled the air.

With all of its strength, a rokuro-kubi's neck is closer to a tentacle than anything else. In fact, it's what they normally use to kill their prey, crushing them slowly. Add the surge of adrenaline she probably got from the burning to that strength and she had no problem wrenching herself from my grip. Which wasn't a big deal. I'd expected that. Burning her was more of a delaying action, really. What I hadn't expected, though, was her flailing into the knife bucket as she pulled away, knocking them all into the fryer.

"Naturally," I grumbled under my breath.

I pulled the fryer basket, filled with knives and extra crispy fries, out of the grease and swung it behind me, expecting to connect with a lot of angry rokuro-kubi head. Grease arced through the empty air and dappled the pristine surface of one of the coolers.

"Well that was anticlimactic," I said.

Then something blunt rammed me in the back, just between my shoulder blades, with enough force to send the fryer basket and its contents flying from my hand and me sprawling on the floor again. I rolled to the side when I landed, causing Theresa to smash her face into the floor instead of my back.

"Graaah!" she screamed through a bloody mouth.

I made out at least three broken teeth in there, but there were probably more. That brought a little smile to my face. I didn't have time to gloat, though. She came at me again, biting and flailing about wildly. I managed to skid away from her snapping teeth, kicking myself across a floor that smelled vaguely of bleach and French fries. A few of those kicks hit her square in the face, but all that did was make her madder. Even breaking her nose with one kick didn't slow her down.

I don't normally admit this, but I was starting to get a little worried. I was running out of floor and really didn't have anything on me to actually kill something with essentially human weaknesses. Until one of the knives came into view, one with a long, serrated blade topping its black handle.

The classics never go out of style.

I grabbed the knife and swung. Theresa reeled her head in, but not quite enough to keep me from nicking the bridge of her nose. The flesh there turned a mottled grey that spread out in a small circle of rot about the size of a penny.

She screamed.

I looked at the knife. It seemed ordinary. No magic, no runes, no weird blessings from some random god or spirit. Just a sharp knife. Made in Japan.

I smiled. "The kami of knives cursed all of you, didn't he?"

She growled. "I will–"

"Do absolutely nothing," I said as I wobbled to my feet. "Or I'll tell the living impaired ladies out there to pelt your defenseless body with butter knives until you rot away. Even the dead stripper should be able to figure out how to pick up a knife."

"I heard that," April said from the dining room.

"You were meant to," I shouted back.

Theresa's head zipped back into the dining room. I followed it, this time going around the counter instead of over it, taking my time.

"What did you do to her?" Betty asked me.

"Kept her from eating me?" I said, not entirely sure where Betty's priorities had drifted to in her deceased years.

"Poor thing," she said to Theresa. "You go wash up and I'll cover your tables for a bit."

I didn't even know where to begin to correct her on that one. Luckily, I didn't have to. Theresa ran for the front door and yanked it open. Light the color of pus seeped its way into the restaurant, causing the floor tiles to smoke wherever it landed and the chrome to tarnish. Sounds I'd only ever heard once, and tried for weeks to forget with large quantities of alcohol, pushed their way in, making every hair on my body stand on end and my muscles tense with the need to run. In the crack of outside that the door reveled, tentacles the size of trees, their flesh grey and sluicing off in rotted sheets, swayed gently to their own rhythm, long strands of yellowish cilia sprouting off of every inch of them, searching the air for anything foolish enough to come too close.

"Don't go out there!" I yelled.

Too late, though. Theresa shot out. I ran for the door and braced myself against it, hating what I knew was coming next. Nobody deserved what was about to happen. Not even someone who'd just tried to eat me.

The pounding came first. Hard and desperate. Then the begging. I couldn't make out what she was saying, but I could tell she was pleading for me to open the door and let her back in. Then, worst of all, the noise stopped.

No one said anything. No one moved. We just waited for what we knew on some instinctual level was coming: the scream, high pitched, hoarse, and abruptly gone.

Betty and April stood there, staring at me, each one holding onto herself to keep from trembling.

"What did you just do?" April asked.

"The door opens up to the spot closest to wherever you're thinking of. Not every place it opens up to is on Earth. It also goes…there."

I'd never heard of Brew's opening onto the Festering Plains, but I wasn't about to let on. Plus, they'd probably hear the shaking in my voice if I had to explain things, and it's never good to let a client see you spooked.

Three polite knocks came from the other side of the door.

"You can't come in," I told the owner of the knock, making damn sure to keep my voice level. "I've got a saint's pinky bone, and I'm not afraid to use it on you."

"Heard," a deep voice cut through my brain. "Rains said. Joys of Amon personified."

"Go away," I said, trying to think of home, which isn't exactly an easy task with a world of demons on the other side of the door politely knocking to be let in. I can only guess what Theresa was thinking that made it open up on a circle of Hell created from the rotting remains of something so far beyond my level of experience that I'd never even heard a name for it.

"Smell your taste. Six souls. Three bodies. Extra for us."

A small line of blood dribbled out of my nose. "No. By the power of Saint Lazarus, I command you to go the hell away. And use your outside voice if you're going to keep talking to me."

"The painter?" it asked out loud. I'd guess there was amusement in its voice, but it was hard to tell. I doubted that anything as subtle as inflection ranked real high on its list of priorities.

"Yes, the painter. When did all of you get so damn snobby about which saints a guy uses?"

"Just one?" it whined.

"No."

Then nothing.

I waited. When nothing kept happening, I stopped leaning into the door. Eventually, I worked up the nerve to open the door a crack and peek outside. Sodium lights buzzed their orange illumination down on a parking lot.

"Are we safe now?" April asked from right behind me, causing me to jump. I'd been so focused on the outside that I wasn't paying attention to the inside.

"Don't do that. And yeah, I think so."

I looked around the diner. "Betty?"

She shot up from beside the remaining waitress. "Yeah, hon?"

"What's her name again?" I asked, nodding to the woman still hiding under the table.

"Diane. She's a nice girl. A bit slow during the rushes, but she's only been here for about three months."

I held up a hand. "Thanks, Betty."

"Diane?" I said in my best things-are-fine voice. "My name's Roger. You can come out now. All the bad stuff's gone."

"Theresa...," she said in a soft voice.

"Was a monster. But she's gone."

"How...how could she be that thing? I worked with her for weeks. She seemed so normal."

"Well, in fairness, I make my living dealing with things like her and she fooled me. So don't feel too bad. Now, Hrothgar's back in the office writing Brew a note about Theresa. Can you go back there and tell him she's gone?"

Diane climbed out from under the table slowly, as if she was expecting another monster to jump out at her. Nothing attempted to eat her, so she smoothed down her apron and went into the kitchen through a back door that I hadn't noticed. Must have been the one Theresa had used to sneak up on me.

I went over to my booth and sat back down. Naturally, my coffee was cold.

"Betty, can you get me another coffee?"

"Sure. Be right back with it."

April sat down. "What just happened?"

"A rokuro-kubi tried to eat me, I fought back, it went to Hell. You were there, too."

"Roger!"

"What do you want me to say? I can't explain every little thing that happens to you. We'd be here all night. Just chalk it up to an occupational hazard."

She crossed her arms. "Fine."

After a couple of minutes of silence, she finally said, "If we're not going to talk about it, then talk about my case. What did that baron guy say? You never told me."

I took a second to calm my nerves and switch mental gears. "That he's an idiot, basically, but I already knew that. He wouldn't tell me what Damballa did or got out of it, though, which really worries me."

"Why? You said he was just the god of snakes. How's that dangerous?"

"He's also the father of all loas, so he's got some power over spirits and ghosts. That aspect should make him a good candidate for helping us with the nagas, but he's always stayed out of it in the past."

Betty came over with another cup of coffee for me, staring intently at it to make sure it didn't literally slip through her fingers. It takes a lot of work, but ghosts can move things if they focus enough on them or if they're in a place that they have enough of a connection to. Luckily, Diane didn't take this opportunity to come back out, or else she would have been back under the table at the sight of a cup of coffee floating through the air.

"Thanks," I told her. "Why don't you go check up on Diane?"

"Sure. They really don't like each other, you know. Hrothgar used to date her room-mate's mom. Well, they broke up, and my goodness was it bad! He –"

I held up a hand. "Betty, just go check on them."

"Gotcha," she said and walked away.

"Why doesn't Damballa help with the nagas?" April asked. Like most ghosts, she was fixated on what was keeping her here.

I took a sip of the fresh coffee. "I really don't know. Damballa's old, even for gods, so his reasoning's a little hard to follow most of the time. He was a strong god in Africa before voodoo came around, and voodoo gave him the chance to become a serious power. Not as big of a player as Yahweh or Kali, but close."

"He's not all scary looking, like a giant snake, is he?" April shuddered. I thought about what to say here. Damballa, like most gods, could appear in whatever form he wanted, and, like most gods, he had his favorite shapes, one of them being an albino snake about the size of a large house. I opted for a half-truth.

"No, he usually shows up as a bald black man with black eyes. He

73

speaks very slowly and deliberately. Some of the gods think it's because he's stupid, but I've heard of him coming up with some pretty amazing things. He stopped one of Anansi's schemes all by himself a few years ago, which takes some doing. I'm more inclined to believe he's one of those rare types of gods – a smart one."

"I thought gods were super-smart, or something," April said. "That's what they say in church, anyway."

"Good P.R," I said with a smile. "They're smart, but only because they're old. Even then, though, most are only a little brighter than your average person since they tend to have problems thinking outside of their function. Which is extremely good, because it means that they can be beaten by an above-average person like me."

"You make it sound like we're playing a game."

I finished off my coffee. "That's what they think it is, so I've got to. It's the best way to stop whatever they're doing."

"Sounds kind of childish."

"You'll get no argument from me. The hardest part of the game, though, is figuring out who's playing and what it takes to keep them from winning."

"Well, we already know who's playing, right? There's the baron guy, Damballa, and the nagas. Now we just need to figure out what they want." April looked down and added quietly, "And why they killed me."

"Oh, I'm sure there are a few other players keeping hidden. There always are. Don't worry, though. I'm here, and I'm the best there is at my job."

"You're the only one there is at your job," April said flatly.

I waved her off with my right hand. "Technicalities."

A plate was set down in front of me. A burger with two patties sat next to a pile of French fries almost spilling onto the floor.

"From Hrothgar," Diane said. "For getting rid of the monster."

Then she disappeared back into the kitchen.

"Aren't you going to thank her?" April asked.

"No, I think she's been traumatized enough tonight. She walked away because she just wants to forget about the whole thing. Pretty normal for most people who wind up seeing this sort of crap. By next week, she'll either have accepted it, or she'll have a new job and put up enough mental barriers that she won't even remember Theresa's name."

"But doesn't –"

"No," I said, holding up a French fry. "No more questions until after I've eaten this wonderful, free, grease-filled food. I'm going to need all my strength to deal with the Fountain."

**5.**

The Fountain was a pool-sized, rectangular water fountain occupying most of the area between Sprau Tower, Miller Auditorium, and Dalton Hall on Western Michigan University's campus. It probably had an actual name, but I'd never bothered to find it out. Never seemed a priority. It was currently empty for the winter, save for a few puddles from the rain, some dead leaves, and various forms of garbage that had gathered in it. The half-light of the area changed its normally neutral blue basin to a decidedly more sinister shade, one very close to that of a drowning victim's skin.

"There's nothing here," April observed.

"Yes and no," I said. "We're not really here for the fountain. We're here for the old bastard that lives in it. He's about as trustworthy as your average crack head, but he's right more often than he's lying to you, so he's worth talking to."

I got up on the fountain's edge, facing the ten-story, Lego-block looking Sprau Tower. "Oh great and knowledgeable Sue," I began, mockingly, "appear before us mere mortals and share your wisdom."

"His name's Sue?" April asked, not sure whether to believe me or not.

"Kind of."

I waited a moment in silence. "I said the words, Sue, now get out here."

"I want the girl to say them," a voice like cracking ice said from the fountain's drains.

"What? No, you old letch. This is serious."

The voice cackled. "Then you better hurry. And she has to use my full name."

"Fine, whatever," I said. "Have it your way."

I motioned for April to step up next to me. "Do you remember what I said?" I asked after she'd joined me.

She nodded. "I think so."

"Good. Just say that, and we can get this show moving."

"What's his full name?"

"Kalamazoo."

"He's named after the city?"

I shook my head. "No, he's the spirit of the Kalamazoo River, and why I don't go swimming anywhere in lower Michigan anymore. For some reason he likes to hang out here. Personally, I think it's because he likes ogling the women that sit on the edge of the fountain."

"Jealous?" the voice in the fountain asked me.

I pointedly didn't answer.

April cleared her throat. "Oh great and knowledgeable Kalamazoo, appear before us mere mortals and share your wisdom."

The nine jets in the fountain's center turned on all at once, spraying water fifteen feet in the air. Gradually, the water collecting in the fountain's basin gathered into one area and rose, shaping itself into a generally human form as it did. As soon as it took a fully human shape, specific features appeared until a twenty foot tall naked old man resolved itself, complete with pot-belly and various sagging parts.

"What do you want?" he asked at last.

"For you to shape some clothes for yourself, for starters," I said, trying not to look below the old man's watery waist. It wasn't as frightening as most naked old people are, but it wasn't much better, either.

"I don't hear your lady-friend complaining," the Kalamazoo River said with a proud smile and a little shake of his hips.

I looked at her. April was just staring. "I don't think it's out of admiration. Looks more like shock to me."

The smile wavered. "Fine."

The river's surface shimmered, and its naked body was replaced by one with a pair of Bermuda shorts, a Hawaiian shirt, and a straw hat. "Better?"

My burger stopped threatening to make a return visit. "Much, thank you."

"Thanks," April managed.

"Now, what do you want?" he repeated. "I've got better things to do than talk to you."

"       I want to know why Damballa reincarnated a naga as a human and where the old snake is," I said.

"Ah, so you've found out about that," the river said, straightening his straw hat. "I guess it was only a matter of time."

I saw no need to expose how late in the game I was entering, so I said, "Yeah, I've known about it for a while now."

The river cackled a bit more. He wagged a finger at me. "Don't lie to a liar, boy. If you'd known about this sooner than probably yesterday, you would've been here before now."

"Or I just don't like talking to you, Old Man River, so I didn't want to come see you unless I had to."

He pointed at me. "Either way, you need me, so show respect."

"Give me a reason to, and I will. Now, answer my questions so I can get out of here."

"The first part's easy. Even you should be able to understand it. Gods need mortal hands to do some of their grunt work. Always have. Really all you monkeys are good for."

"Yeah, yeah, we're primates, ook ook. Between you and the Fae that insult's lost a lot of its punch, Sue. Find some new material." The king and queen of Faerie used to call me their favorite monkey. Until the little incident between me and their daughter. Now they mostly refer to me as "Kill him" and "Cut his head off."

"So what's the naga doing for him?" I asked.

"Oh, a little of this, a little of that."

"Quit being coy. We both know modesty isn't one of your faults."

"Use your head, Detective," he snapped. "What does the herald of a god usually do?"

"Ah."

"Ah?" April asked. "Ah what? What's he doing?"

"Preparing the way for Damballa to end the world."

"How?"

I shrugged. "Psyching up the faithful, preparing the rituals, lighting the special candles. Could be anything. He probably killed you as part of it. A lot of rituals go a lot smoother with a human sacrifice added in."

"That's the brilliance that explains why the city chose you as Detective," Sue sniped.

"If you can get it to pick somebody else, then be my guest," I said.

"Until then, we're stuck with each other. Now, where's Damballa so I can get this whole thing over with and go to bed?"

Sue crossed his arms and looked away from us. "Find him yourself. That's enough freebies for one night."

Water spirits can be such divas. Without fail, any conversation with Sue wound up at this point. He'd answer a few minor questions, then get standoffish with the big ones. I'd gotten used to it, but it didn't make it any less irritating.

"Get to the point, piss stream," I said. "What do you want?"

He looked at us out of the corner of an eye. "A kiss from your girlie."

As far as demands went, this one was pretty modest. Last time I'd needed information from him he'd wanted the paper mill shut down for good. I talked him down to a week, and pulled some strings to have the place closed for safety inspections.

April narrowed her eyes. "I'm not his girlie."

He turned and squatted uncomfortably close to us, bringing with him the moldy smell of brackish water. "Whore, special friend, moll, whatever you are, I want a kiss or I'm not helping."

"You really know how to sweet talk the ladies," I said.

"You should be grateful that I'm even asking, Detective. In the old days, when my kin and I were still wild things, I'd abduct a woman for as long as she amused me, then let the body float into Lake Michigan." He laughed without any real feeling. "Now we're all confined to one path, one bed. We're tame. We hardly kill anyone anymore."

"Yeah, so sorry you had to give up your serial rapist murderer days," I said flatly.

"How many women did you do that to?" April asked, her eyes huge with shock.

"How should I know? It's not like they were important. They were just humans," he responded.

"When this is all over, you and I are going to have a talk, Sue," I told him. Then, to April, "Give Ted Bundy here his kiss so we can get going,"

"Fine," April growled. "But just a small one. And no tongue."

"And you have to shrink down to human size," I added.

"Yes, yes," he said, water draining away from his form until he was no more than six feet tall.

Sue made a production of wiping his lips, then licking them. He held out his arms. "Pucker up."

April bent down and, just as she was about to kiss his fishy lips, moved to the side and kissed him on the cheek, sending delicate ripples latticing through his form from where her lips touched.

"There," she said.

Sue instantly reared back, growing to his full height, rage contorting the river's face and sending mini waves crashing across his surface. "You call that a kiss?"

"Never try out-cunning a stripper in matters of negotiable physical affection," I said, laughing at him. "Now, where's Damballa?"

"I'd tell you, if just to get rid of you faster," the river spirit said, his form settling down to a slow roil. "But the gentlemen behind you may have a problem with that."

April and I turned. I recognized the college kid standing behind us from earlier in the evening, but knew it was better not to let on. He had on frayed jeans, a black T-shirt, and a scuffed-up, black leather jacket. He also had something I couldn't quite identify for a moment.

"The reincarnated naga?" I asked him.

"Yeah," the kid said. "And you're this Roger guy I keep hearing about, right?"

I nodded. "And I'm willing to bet you already know April." I motioned to her with my head.

The kid looked right at her. "She's the stripper we killed the other night. So?"

"So she's not too happy about it. She looked me up. When I was just about to go to sleep, I might add. So now I'm not too happy about it."

"Poor baby," the river said from behind me.

"Shut up, Sue," I said over my shoulder. "I'm not too happy with you right now, either, piss stream."

"And I'm not too happy with you and your race," he replied in a voice of anger that only most gods can manage. "Dumping chemicals and waste and garbage in me. It'll be a relief to be rid of all of you."

"Except for our skater snake here?" I asked.

"And any others that —"

"Shut up, river," the kid ordered.

"Are you going to let him talk to you like that?" I asked the river without taking my eyes off the kid.

"If it gets rid of you, I'll get down on my knees and give him a blowjob."

The kid visibly shuddered at this notion.

"I'd pay to see that," I said to no one in particular.

April stared at me. "That's gross."

I shrugged. "I've seen worse. The old Greek supernaturals would–"

"I'll take your word for it," April interrupted with a look of disgust.

"Who grew your fancy new body?" I asked the kid. "I don't recognize the handiwork, so I'm guessing someone who's on the way out."

"He was until he signed up with us. Not that it'll matter to you in a few minutes, but Glykon made my body." The kid made a show of looking himself over. "Did a good job, too. For a human god. I've been able to do all sorts of stuff with it the last few years."

"Never heard of him," I admitted. "But I do like the dreads. Gives you that pot-head look that's all the rage today."

"Whatever, dead man. I've heard all about your attitude. It ain't gonna save you here, bro."

"Anyway. Is this going to be a chase scene? Because it's late, and I'd like to get it going if it's going to be."

"Only if you're dumb enough to run."

Two nagas, one the rust and tan of the one I'd run into earlier that evening, the other deep black with a grey stomach, leapt out of the kid to stand on either side of him. "He's all yours."

I didn't see them fully materialize. April and I were already running the two hundred or so yards to the circle drive where the Sunbird was parked. It wasn't necessary for me to turn to see what was after me. I could feel them coming. I could also sense that April was falling behind.

"Dammit, you're dead," I shouted. "You can run faster than that."

"Run, Detective," Sue shouted, cackling. "Go find your death."

April began to catch up. Unfortunately, so did the nagas. I could tell that they were going to overtake us before we reached the Sunbird, so I reached into my pocket and pulled out Floyd.

"Sorry, Floyd," I said as I rubbed my fingernail over part of the inscription, breaking the binding spell. "I really was going to let you go at a better time, but if it comes down to you or me, it's gotta be you."

I threw Floyd behind me. When the urinal cake landed, the ghost of Floyd in his real, scrawny form appeared with his greasy black hair. He looked around just in time to see the nagas leap on him. He got out a quick,

"You basta –" before they tore him to shreds, which they quickly devoured

I ran around the Sunbird, opened the door, and started it up, leaving my door open just long enough to let April slip past the wards. I peeled out as soon as she got in, the force of the forward momentum closing the door for me. The nagas were still following.

"Give it up," I said, watching them in the mirror as I pulled away.

A yellow Mustang in the parking lot we were passing started up and raced toward us. It was on the other side of a grassy divider, but it barreled over it, missing the Sunbird by inches.

"You've got to be kidding," I said.

We hurtled down the curving road leading to West Michigan Avenue, the Sunbird's tires screaming the entire time. I narrowly avoided a red and white Ranger as we ran the stop sign and turned onto the road.

"Where are we going?" April screamed.

"Hell if I know. I'm just trying to keep us, me, alive."

We ran the light, thankfully devoid of traffic, and continued down West Michigan. The Mustang shot up beside us. Black metal flashed dully at me from the small pistol its driver pointed at me. The driver was a woman, but I couldn't make out her features in the dark. I slowed just enough to turn down a side-street without shooting over the sidewalk. The other car sped past, but I heard it screech a sharp U-turn and head back toward us.

"We'll try to hide out in one of the condo buildings back here," I said. "With luck she'll pass right by us."

"Don't you have a gun?" April asked. "Just shoot her if she comes by."

"I do, but I'd rather not. I don't need any more ghosts hanging around me, thanks."

"What if you're the ghost?"

"Good point."

We pulled into the far parking lot of a condo complex. In an ideal world, it would've been packed with other cars, leaving one space open for mine to slide into, frustrating our hunter enough to give up on the chase. This world being far from ideal, there were five other cars. I parked between the only two sitting near each other –a rusting, blue SUV and what looked like a brand new, green pick-up truck – hoping it would be enough to conceal us, but not counting on it. I clicked the engine off, ducked down, and reached over into the glove compartment for my shiny .38.

"I've only fired this thing a couple of times," I told her, "so don't expect it to save us."

In less than a minute, the low growl of a Mustang's engine rolled up behind the Sunbird.

"How the hell did she find us so fast?" I asked.

It pulled to a stop behind us, blocking the Sunbird in. A door opened slowly and closed. Footsteps clicked toward us.

I sighed. "Might as well get this over with."

I threw my door open and jumped out, pulling the gun's trigger. This would have been more impressive if the safety hadn't still been on.

"Dammit!" I screamed as I ran to the front of the SUV and crouched down, only just getting out of the way of a bullet.

"We always thought you more impressive, Detective," the woman said in a voice that, despite its dry harshness, I immediately recognized.

"And I thought you lizards were at least a little more original than this," I said back. I flicked the safety off.

"Hello, spirit," the woman said to April from the passenger's side. "Stay. I will take care of you soon."

April screamed. Understandable, given that the woman shooting at me was her, or, more specifically, her naga-possessed corpse.

I peeked over the SUV's hood and shot twice, putting two holes in the formerly new truck, then ducked back down.

"Poor Detective. He cannot even fire a gun. I can, though." She shot twice into the SUV's side. The bullets came out inches from my head. "I have spent the last five centuries possessing your weak little bodies, using them to shoot as many of your kind as I could. I am quite good at it."

Footsteps came to the front of my car. I scooted around to the other side of the SUV.

Lights began coming on in windows.

"Jump into the body," I told April.

"What?" she said, still in shock from seeing her own body walking around without her in it.

"Just do it! I don't have time to argue with you!"

A door to one of the near condos opened and a man in a blue bathrobe stepped out with a shotgun.

"What the hell's going on out here?" he shouted.

The thing in April's corpse shot him once in the head. His body fell down, leaving a fairly startled ghost standing where it had been.

I half-stood, shot twice, missing both times, and crouched down again.

"Do it or people are going to die," I shouted at April.

She ghosted out of my car and through the SUV. A moment later, the body screamed and its gun clattered to the sidewalk.

I stood. April's corpse shook violently, causing the spirit inside it to lose enough control that the head fell to the side on its broken neck.

I walked slowly to the once pretty, but now purple and slightly desiccated, body. "It was a good idea to use whichever of you is in April's body to find us," I said, "but really stupid to actually come after us in it. Or has it been so long since you've had a body that you've forgotten that her spirit would try to kick out whatever was in the body if she jumped in?"

I shot out the corpse's knees, causing it to fall to the ground, then crouched down next to it. "Now, I'm going to be nice and let you out of this body you've so thoughtfully bound yourself to. But not for a bit."

I went to the Sunbird's trunk and opened it, then came back, picked up April's body, and tossed it in next to some jumper cables, a spare tire, and a red tool box.

"All right, April. You can come out now."

April's ghost sat up and walked over to me. I closed the trunk on her body as it tried to sit up, too, knocking it down. Hard. Loud pounding immediately began rattling the lid as the naga tried using April's corpse as a battering ram, oblivious to any damage it would cause the body.

"Is it going to ghost out?" April asked.

"No. Possessing a dead body that way's great for getting physical again for a while, but it sucks if you want to go back to being a ghost. You have to bind yourself to it, and the only way to break the binding is to destroy the heart.

"Don't worry, though" I said through the trunk, "I'll let you out in about ten minutes."

"You're going to let that…thing go?" April asked. "It stole my body, and you're just going to let it go?"

"Trust me," I said with a smile as I walked over to the Mustang.

The inside of the car had the lived-in feel to it that I expected from strippers and salesmen. Judging by the red purse and pile of multicolored lacey things in the backseat, not to mention the lei hanging from the rearview mirror, stripper seemed most likely.

"Shouldn't we leave? I mean, won't there be cops and stuff soon?"

I stepped back from the Mustang with the purse. "It'll take a while for them to get here."

I walked to my car, rummaging through the purse. Eventually, I pulled out April's ID, then tossed the purse in the passenger's seat and got in. "We can go now. I just wanted to grab your purse real quick. No need to connect you with this just yet."

"Thank you," she said, getting in and sitting on the purse. "I didn't think you cared that much."

"Don't get all misty-eyed on me...," I looked at her ID. "Sara Marie Goode. Nice name, by the way. Much better than your stripper name."

"Hey!"

"Just curious about the real name of the person I'm working for."

"I'd better not end up in a urinal cake," April warned, some fear in her voice.

"Or what? You'll hang around in my closet again?" I started the car and drove up on the sidewalk to get out. "Don't worry. As long as you don't do anything to tick me off too badly you should be urinal cake free."

*   *   *   *

"I'm willing to bet you know where we are," I said through the Sunbird's trunk approximately five minutes later. I'd left April in the car.

"I will kill you when you open this lid," April's body said.

"You'll try, I don't doubt that. But I know something you don't."

I opened the trunk and shot April's body in the elbows. "I know when I'm going to open the trunk."

April's body lunged at me, biting like a bad horror movie zombie. I stepped to the side, letting it continue its arc uninterrupted and fall headfirst onto the road. A nasty sounding crunch, probably from the nose breaking, brought out an involuntary cringe from me when it landed.

"Now, if you'll look to your right, you'll see the Evil House." I motioned to it. "So named because it's about the most terrifying thing in this city, next to a little Thai place I know in the mall."

This was a bit of an exaggeration. If I had to be brutally honest, my office was the most terrifying place in the city. Over the years, the various Detectives had gathered a truly impressive collection of awful things that they couldn't, or wouldn't, destroy. The Throne of Brigid, God's Dictionary, and the Seed of Kalamazoo, to name just a few of the things that made me

85

hate going there.

The body somehow struggled to its knees and looked like it was about to try for another lunge. I was right about the nose, which now hung from the corpse's face by only a few bits of skin, giving me a clear view of April's grey and rotted nasal cavity.

I pointed my gun at the its heart. "Try it. Even I can't miss at this range. Any last words?"

"I will come back from Sraatsa," April's corpse said. "I will kill you, Detective."

"If that's giant lizard-thing Hell, then I seriously doubt it." I shot the body in its heart. It fell back onto the road with a satisfying thump.

A naga, red with a tan stomach, stood up from the body. It hissed and drew its arm back as if to claw out my throat, but stopped and lowered it. Slowly, its face slack and eyes empty, it turned and walked into the Evil House.

I picked up April's body, tossed it back in the trunk, and closed it. Then I got in my car and drove away as fast as I could.

"Was that revenge enough for you?" I asked April after we were driving.

"Will it suffer in there?"

"Beats me. One can always hope."

"What about my body?" April asked.

"I was going to molest it a bit and then make a mask out of the skin."

Nothing but stunned silence came from her.

"Relax," I said, smiling. "I'm kidding. We're going to make a stop at my office, and then we'll take it over to the cemetery across from Kalamazoo College and toss it on a new grave. It'll be found in the morning and buried sometime after the cops have had their investigation into the theft and defilement of your body."

As much as I hated actually going to that cemetery, it was convenient for body disposal. Kalamazoo's chief of police, a guy named Carlson, and I had a deal, one that he'd had with the previous Detective: any bodies that I found in relation to my job, I'd dump there, then call him and let him know what happened. Gave the families some closure and kept me out of jail.

April looked at the back seat as if she could see through it to her body. "It was horrible in there. So cold and stiff, like I'd been frozen."

"Well, your body has been dead for a while. What'd you expect?"

"And I saw what they did to it to keep it…up."

"Killed and ate bums, right?" I guessed as I turned onto Lovell Street. "Kind of standard practice for animated corpses to keep them fresh."

"After they…" April trailed off.

"Seduced them," I finished. "I guess they killed and ate desperate, mostly blind bums."

"Would you shut up!" she yelled at me. "You're talking about my body!"

"Which nearly killed me and did kill some poor schlub who probably didn't do much worth living for, let alone dying for. If you weren't here, I'd burn the damn thing out of principle."

"Principle?" April asked, getting angrier. "What principles do you even have?"

"The 'you don't shoot at me and continue existing in one piece' principle."

April put her hands up and shook her head. "Let me out."

"You're a ghost. Just stand up," I said, getting tired once again of her whining. I expected some griping from the recently dead, but this was getting tedious.

"Fine, I will. And I'll find someone else to help me."

I winked at her. "Good luck with that, hon. The nearest person that does what I do is in Detroit. Better get walking."

April sat back in the seat and crossed her arms, pouting.

The rest of the trip was pleasantly quiet.

*　　　　*　　　　*　　　　*

"I've got to warn you, my office is a bit of a mess," I told April as we stood in front of the smoked glass entrance. "It's got a poltergeist in it that refuses to leave things where they are."

April, still upset about her body, didn't even look at me. "It can't be any worse than your apartment," she said with little emotion.

"You'd think so, wouldn't you?"

I opened the door and turned on the lights, which only just made it through a dusty haze that sandstorms would envy. The vague smell of blood lilted through the air, always just at the back of my nose, like it was lying low, waiting to mug me when my defenses were down. An all too real possibility, since I'd never found where it was coming from. Two desks, both buried under enough books, papers, and files to recreate a small deciduous forest, sat facing each other from opposite walls. Great tottering pillars of paper rose up from parts of the room like someone had attempted to create a model of Stonehenge out of paperwork. Across from the door, nearly hidden by two overflowing bookcases, was the only window outside. Dusty shades covered it, possibly because the string to raise them was behind one of the bookcases. There was a close, wooden door on the wall to our left. As usual, my feet tingled from all of the supernatural crap in the basement, some of it chained there and in one case pressed under one hundred pounds of blessed silver in the shape of Solomon's seal.

I fought back the urge to go check on everything down there. No need to let April in on any of the truly terrifying relics a hundred-plus years of Detectives had hidden away from pretty much the entire world.

Besides, I had other things to worry about. The overwhelming power emanating from the basement effectively cancelled out my "gift," making me have to rely only on what I saw. And I didn't like what I saw. No papers or books were flying through the air to hit me, which was unusual given that that seemed to be the office poltergeist's main way of saying hello. Carefully, we stepped in.

Curious in spite of herself, April looked around the room. "What's that?" she asked, looking at the door.

"Bathroom. Now shush. Something's wrong. I locked the door before I left."

The sound of a toilet flushing came from the bathroom and the door opened. The man who walked out had to duck slightly to keep from hitting his bald head on the door-frame. Empty, black eyes looked at me from a smiling face. He adjusted the jacket of a red suit so immaculately tailored that it looked closer to being another layer of skin than clothing.

April hid behind me. I just shook my head tiredly. "Evening, Damballa. Y'know, I don't even know why I bother locking the door. It's not like it keeps anyone out."

"Anticipated earlier," he said in a slow, scratchy voice that made him sound like a professional chain-smoker. Far as I knew, he always spoke in short, breathy phrases, elongating the vowels as if he was almost out of air. Like every syllable cost him something to utter. Or like he just didn't feel something as important as words should be wasted on the likes of me.

"What can I say? I've never been big on punctuality."

Damballa walked casually across the room, his tall, thin frame making him look like a particularly well-dressed giraffe striding through off-white and manila colored trees.

"That's close enough. Not very bright of you, showing up in my place of power uninvited. Tell me what you want before I do something unpleasant to you."

Damballa shrugged and spread his hands in front of him. "See how you are. Been some time."

"That's what happens when you get banished."

"Small thing. Nature of magik. Allows escape clause. Found this one's. Spiritualist wouldn't understand."

"Detective, Snake Boy," I said casually, not wanting to show any sign of weakness. "I've even got the trench coat to prove it."

"As you say." Then, as if it were an after-thought, "Killed Vesta today."

"Yeah, imagine that, a god with sense. Unlike most of your kind, she knew when her time was up."

I'd apparently struck a nerve of some sort with this comment because anger flashed for just a second across Damballa's face, making it elongate slightly and begin to grow scaly, almost like a naga's. It quickly reverted to human. "Do not put me together with your gods. I am not of them."

Which showed just how angry I'd made him. I'd never heard him say two sentences that complete in a row.

"They aren't my gods. If I were making them, they'd be a lot smarter. They wouldn't try to end the world, for instance."

Damballa smiled hugely, showing his overly white, pointed teeth. "No. Remaking it. Paradise again."

"Paradise for who? Humans or big lizards?"

"All worshippers."

"Well, four of your worshippers just tried to send me on to paradise. Mind explaining that one?"

"Having fun. Nerves. You are not to be hurt. They know this."

I stepped aside from the doorway. "Their fun got a man killed."

"You were not hurt."

"Not from lack of them trying." I motioned to the door. "Now, if you don't mind, I need to work on stopping whatever it is you've got going. And, if I'm very lucky, killing you."

He nodded deeply. "Of course. Must be true to natures. You will fail.

Will help me."

"Like hell I will."

Damballa strode to the door and stopped. He looked at me, then seemed to look through me. "See you both again. Later this morning."

I nodded to the door. "I think that can be arranged. Which would you rather be turned into after I skin you, a pair of boots or a briefcase?"

"Until later." Damballa left, whistling a tune that I couldn't identify.

I shut the door. "Well, that was fun."

April stepped around in front of me. "Fun? How was that fun? I couldn't even move!"

"Damballa can do that to ghosts. It's one of his things. But yeah, I know what you mean. Most gods I would've kept talking, but he's something else. Especially with that little invitation at the end."

"Do you think he meant it?"

I thought for a moment. "Yeah, I do. He probably wants me there to gloat when he does whatever it is he's doing. I only wish I knew how I'm supposed to help. It'd give me more of an idea of how to stop it."

"What do you mean?"

"There's the chance that if I just leave him be, his end-of-the-world scheme won't work. Something a little demon dog told me earlier makes me think Damballa might actually need me there to pull off his ritual. Unfortunately, I can't take that risk."

"Why didn't you just stick him in a urinal cake or something like you and Beth were saying you would?"

"That was what we in the business call 'talking shit.' I could've done some minor stuff since he was here without my permission, but Damballa's way too big league for us to do much to him without some serious power."

A stack of papers rose off of the desk nearest us and moved itself to the other desk, somehow managing not to tumble off.

April's eyes widened. "What just did that?"

I walked over to the spot the papers had previously occupied and examined it. A manila folder labeled "Damballa" sat there. "I told you earlier: the office has a poltergeist. Luckily it seems more aware than the average poltergeist. Sometimes it's even helpful."

"Why can't I see it?"

"Because it's a poltergeist, not a ghost. It never had a body, so it doesn't manifest one like ghosts."

I picked up the folder and opened it. Several handwritten pages filled it, some yellowed with age, the ink eating through the paper.

"What's that?"

"All the information Kalamazoo's Detectives put together on Damballa," I said, leafing through it. "Goes back over a century."

"Why were all of the Detectives men?" April asked, noticing the poor handwriting that each Detective seemed to have. "Except that newer one."

"That newer one is mine."

April smiled. "You have girlie handwriting."

"I have elegant handwriting," I said defensively. "There's a difference. And I don't know why all of the Detectives have been men. Maybe the thing that picks us for the job just likes handsome guys."

I saw that April was about to say something. "Shut up."

"I wasn't going to –"

"Yes, you were." I closed the file. "We can review this later. For now, let's find out who or what the hell Glykon is."

April wrinkled her nose. "Are you going to use some ugly looking book written in blood on human skin?"

"You've been watching way too many horror movies."

I went to the other side of the desk I was standing by and pulled open one of its drawers. After digging through several yellowing books that had been shoved into it, I finally pulled out a white paperback. "Those moldering old things are for amateurs who're more worried about the look of the thing. They work and all, but I'll take a modern reference book any day. A lot less risk of losing your soul."

I quickly found the 'G' section and turned to Glykon.

"Huh."

April came over to me and looked over my shoulder. "Who's Asklepiós?"

"Well, apparently he's an earlier version of Glykon. I always thought he was just a washed-up god of healing who panhandled at the coffee shop down the street."

I flipped back in the book and looked up Asklepiós. "That explains it. He used to be a snake god of some kind. Probably why he was okay with working with Damballa. And according to some myths, he was known to bring people back from the dead for gold. Got him killed by Zeus at least once."

I tossed the book back in the drawer, then went over to the other desk and opened one of its drawers. A tangle of charms, runes, daggers, and various holy and unholy symbols filled it. Normally, it's a really bad idea to keep random minor magic things in a jumbled mess in a drawer, but they all seemed to keep each other in check as long as no one bled on them or burned strong incense too close. Sure, there was the occasional puff of black, sulfurous flame or flash of sugar cookie-scented, pearlescent light, but I put that down as just a natural discharge. Kind of like static electricity for the soul. I delicately picked through everything until I found what I needed.

"I never like using this thing," I said, holding up a dagger with an iron handle and a six-inch obsidian blade that glinted dully in the office's light. "I always feel dirty."

"It's a knife," April said without much enthusiasm.

"Actually, it's a very sharp dagger. More importantly for us, it's a symbol of death and big, gaping wounds. Makes it a good opposite of healing and therefore perfect for threatening a god of healing with. You ready?"

"To do what? Pick on a bum that used to be a god?"

"Pretty much."

*     *     *     *

If I were a betting man, I would've bet that Asklepiós, or Glykon, or whatever he was calling himself now, still had some kick left in him. Creating a fresh body for the naga was proof of that. Not that you could tell by looking at him. Asklepiós had seen better days. At least, I hoped he had. The layers of rotting and filthy clothes clinging to him looked older than me and gave the impression that he'd just kept adding pieces as others disintegrated. Poultices for his clothing, I guess. And for a god of healing, he was looking less than healthy. Rotted teeth, yellow eyes, and uneven, greasy hair were not terms I'd ever expected to use to describe a god of healing. We found him where I'd expected to, begging for change on the sidewalk outside of Zevon's Warren, the coffee shop just down the street from my office.

Zevon's Warren occupied a special place in Kalamazoo's secret history, depending upon who you listened to. Jakobar, in his more lucid moments, swore that it was piece of his native timeline. Tapestry, the Animated Man, would tell stories about the secret inks that'd been used to illustrate its walls and give it protection from everything short of the sun going supernova. The files of the Detectives called it by its other name, The Grey Man's Retreat, and said it was the only truly neutral territory in

Kalamazoo. I'd never run into anyone calling himself the Grey Man, but I could attest to the last story, having seen things sharing a cup of coffee behind its brick walls that, everywhere else, tried to kill each other on sight. Made it the perfect hiding place for a down-on-his-luck god.

"Spare some change, mister?" Asklepiós said through blackened teeth and a cloud of cheap liquor mean enough it probably had its own criminal record.

"No, not tonight," I told him. "And stop with the 'mister' thing. You know who I am and why I'm here."

He cackled, then pulled a bottle out from somewhere and took a swig. "Snakes!" he shouted.

"Yeah, snakes," I said, hoping he wasn't talking about a hallucination. "Look, I need you to focus past the lighter fluid you're drinking and talk to me for a second. Can you do that for me?"

"This is pointless," April complained, hugging herself. "Just threaten him with the knife so we can get out of here. He's creeping me out."

"Pretty," Asklepiós said, looking at her.

"And dead," I said. "Damballa had her killed for some reason."

His eyes shot back to me. "Dan-aido-hwedo?"

The word sounded familiar, but it took a moment to click that I'd seen it in the file on Damballa. It was his African name. "Yeah. Him. You did a job for him. Made a body for a naga and let Baron Samedi put its soul in. Remember?"

"For belief!" he shouted. He danced in a circle, repeating the phrase loudly.

I grabbed his shoulders once he was facing me again. His clothes were warm to the touch, and their smell had an oily life of its own that threatened to fill my lungs and take up permanent residence. "Yeah. Why'd he want it?"

I believed the Fountain's explanation but, given our history, felt the need to dig a little deeper. He'd never give me the whole truth willingly.

"For belief!" he shouted again. He tried to spin away, but I held on tight.

"We got that. You're getting belief out of it. How, though?"

Asklepiós cackled some more and shook his head. "No, no. Dan-aido-hwedo said no. Can't tell."

I sighed. "All right, I tried the nice way."

I let go of him and pulled the dagger out. His reaction was

93

instantaneous. Faster than any human could, he scuttled back from me. He wasn't looking where he was going, though, and ran into the coffee shop's wall with a solid thud, causing him to drop his liquor bottle. It shattered on the sidewalk, freeing more of the liquor's eye-watering stench.

"Safe here!"

I ran up to him while he was figuring out what had happened and put the knife to his throat. "You're only safe inside, Asklepiós. Outside, you're fair game. And for what it's worth, I really didn't want to do this this way. You seem like a harmless enough guy."

He squirmed a bit as the skin near the dagger began to redden. "Hurts!"

"Answer my questions and I'll stop. It's that simple. And sober up, while you're at it. I know you've got enough power left in you to do that at least."

Asklepiós nodded. I stepped back but kept the dagger in plain sight.

The god's clothing began to ripple slowly and fall away in pieces. The skin that I could see grew pale, and a milky film spread over his eyes. Clumps of hair drifted to the ground and tumbled away when the wind picked up.

"What's he doing?" April asked.

"Healing himself," I replied. "He's shedding his skin."

A split appeared down the center of his scalp. He reached up to it and pulled, revealing clean, pale white skin beneath. Slowly, a bald, naked, Greek man emerged as he shuffled off everything that he'd been.

"Wow," April said. I wasn't sure if she was marveling at his penis, his muscular physique, or his regeneration.

"Detective," Asklepiós said as he stepped out of the pile of discarded skin and clothes, his color darkening to its natural hue. "I don't appreciate being threatened."

"And I don't like being treated like I'm some kind of amateur, so we're even."

"What do you want?"

"To know what the hell's going on."

"You already know that. Your world is going to end tonight."

I narrowed my eyes. "Do I have to point the knife at you? What's going on?"

"Dan-aido-hwedo, Damballa to you, is going to bring back the nagas, replacing your race. He promised me worship in a new pantheon if I aided him."

That was a new one. Killing everyone but the faithful or convincing the world to worship him was the standard motivation for a god to go doomsday. Reviving a dead race and replacing humanity with it, though... That was crazy on a whole new level.

"How?"

Asklepiós shook his head. "I...do not know. He wouldn't tell me."

I laughed. "Of course he wouldn't. You're just a hired goon."

I shook my head. "You couldn't just admit you'd had a good run and go out like Vesta, could you? You had to get in on the first get-rich-quick scheme that popped up, even one that most demons would cringe at."

The god looked away.

"Yeah, you should be ashamed. You're a god of healing, and you're helping to commit murder. Hell, forget murder, you're helping commit genocide."

He turned and glared at me. "You have –"

"No idea what it's like? No right to judge you?" I stepped closer to him. "I have every right. It's my race you're trying to kill off, remember? And I've dealt with your kind enough to know exactly what you're going through. It's called old age. Happens to everyone and sucks a lot sometimes. But it gives you no right to pull this kind of shit. You want to feel better? Buy an RV like everyone else."

I dropped the dagger at his feet and turned to leave. "Do the right thing," I said as I walked away.

"That was pretty harsh," April said from just behind me. "The guy was just trying to stay alive."

And with that, April confirmed a few suspicions.

"Him trying to stay alive resulted in you getting killed by the nagas, remember?"

"Oh. Yeah," she said, anger appearing in her voice.

I sighed. "We might as well check out the Warren while we're here. Maybe somebody knows more about what's going on."

$$*\qquad*\qquad*\qquad*$$

Imagine the first bar ever: two cavemen getting together over a flat rock, throwing back slugs of fermented banana juice or whatever the hell cavemen drank, and talking about their mates or children or who got eaten by a leopard last time the bright thing in the sky jumped up from where it hides.

Add to that a cup of Nile delta beer that the slaves drank in dusty rooms to forget they were going to be tossed alive into the pyramid with Pharaoh, a few drams of Greek wine imbibed among tame forests by philosophers to aid in their discussion of Forms, and a mug of honeyed mead guzzled by Vikings in their warm halls to keep back winter's six month chill. Then add a splash of coffee house in the form of comfortable couches. Toss in one central pillar made of some pale wood holding it all up, and that'll give a start on the Warren's interior.

"It just…," April began, looking up and up and up at level upon level of wall-less rooms, their floors only supported by flights of stairs. Vines dangled over the edges of a couple of forested rooms, sand or snow trickled down from one or two others, and the occasional fox peeked over the edge of one room about three quarters of the way up. Somewhere up at the very top, a yellow half-moon shown down on us through an open roof and the foliage of one of the uppermost rooms.

"Goes on forever?" I finished. "Not quite, but it definitely shouldn't fit in a one story building whose longest side is twenty feet. Near as I can tell, whoever owns the place has enough power to keep shoving new rooms into it every age or so. And that's a short list."

Kalamazoo's an origami town. About a third of the city's total area consists of big pockets of reality folded into little spaces. The Temple of the Lost God, the 4D Bar, the Lost Woods, all them are hidden away someplace. There's even rumors of a whole other city stuffed away someplace, though I've never seen any real proof. Doesn't mean it isn't out there, waiting to do something horrible.

"No, this isn't right," she said. "I was just here a month ago with Andrea and Veronica. It was just a regular coffee shop then."

"Defensive glamours. Regular folks walk in, and that's what they see. You're dead, so you're a bit beyond being fooled by illusions. And I'm the city's Detective, so I'm exempt from them."

I scanned the ground floor, hoping that someone useful would be there so I wouldn't have to climb any stairs. It had gotten late enough that the human crowd consisted of one college kid who'd fallen asleep on the orange couch by the front entrance, whatever book he'd been reading still open and clutched on his lap. The non-human crowd was actually pretty sparse, too, a rarity given that at least two-thirds of them were nocturnal. Which worried me. Meant that word had gotten out and they were scared enough to take cover. Timmy the Sin-Eater, scrawny and scarred, sat at his usual spot near the window, nursing a mocha. Every now and then he'd twitch and shrink into himself, realize what he was doing, and jolt upright. Larry, the mad poetry god, hunched over a piece of paper on the other side of the room, scribbling feverishly. Occasionally, a word would flash blue on the paper then float up into the air to evaporate like a smoke ring, and I'd suddenly know "plove" was the word for the smell of purple. Bacchus, Greek god of wine and partying, and Lugh, Celtic god of pretty much whatever he wanted, argued amicably next to a patch of decorative plants, sipping shots of espresso out of apparently bottomless cups. They'd seen the future of beverages centuries back and invested heavily in coffee, making them among the wealthiest gods on the planet. Why they hung out in Kalamazoo as much as they did was beyond me. Both wore immaculately tailored suits. Bacchus's was a dark purple, its jacket designed to hide his enormous stomach and its pants designed to hide, as best it could, his eternal erection. Lugh's suit matched the grey of cold iron and had a bulk to it that made it resemble

armor more than fashion wear. Both gods sported full, neatly manicured black beards.

I generally didn't have a problem with Bacchus. I'd even gone drinking with him once or twice. Possibly more. You didn't always remember times spent with him. Sometimes you didn't even remember your name until you took a hard look at your driver's license and waited for the ability to read to come back. Lugh I only knew in passing and from notes that the other Detectives had kept. Their general opinion was that he tended to be a bit of a hard-ass, but seemed to be an okay god.

"Gentlemen," I said as I walked up to them. "How is everything?"

"Fine, fine," Bacchus said. Then he saw April and perked up. "And who is this lovely creature?"

"April. She's my newest client."

Bacchus took her hand and kissed it. "Charmed."

April let out a little giggle. "Thank you."

"Don't let him fool you," I said. "Bacchus is a bigger letch than the river. He's just more subtle about it and he'll sleep with anything female with a pulse."

Bacchus seemed like he was about to argue the point, then just shrugged. "There might be some truth to that."

I raised an eyebrow. "I once saw you seduce a sixty-year-old woman with a fuller beard than yours. And a hump."

97

"Everyone needs love, Roger. Even if it's only for the night."

"I guess. So, what are you two doing?"

"I'm trying to get Lugh here to admit that he's wrong."

Lugh shook his head. "I simply do not see another option," he said with a slightly French accent. It's a long story why an Irish god has a French accent. Don't ask.

"That's because for a patron of artists you're about as creative as this table," Bacchus said.

"Me? What do your followers do with the gift of wine? Do they compose poems or create sculptures? No. They get drunk out of their senses and go marauding about the countryside, killing, eating, and having sex with anything and anyone that moves."

"All right guys," I said, "enough with 'I've got a secret.' What are you talking about?"

"Oh, Lugh says that we have to kill you to keep Damballa from destroying everything. Don't worry, though, Roger. I won't let him kill you. I say we should just lock you in a cellar or something until the snake gets bored and slithers away. That way everyone wins."

"It is nothing personal, you understand," Lugh said. "You have been a perfectly adequate Detective."

"Thank you?" I said.

"But you are in over your head this time," Lugh continued.

"Yes, the snakes are going to get you. My priestesses have seen it."

"No offense, Bacchus, but I've got prophecies coming out of every major orifice right now, so you'll excuse me if I don't trust the predictions of a bunch of women who are so high they don't know what year it is, let alone anything about the future."

Lugh stood up. A subtle glow of white light began to form around him. "No, they are correct in this case. We have to be safe."

I didn't move. "Better gods than you have tried it."

"Unlikely." Lugh's suit expanded and straightened, forming a suit of flat grey, plate-mail armor, emblazoned with a sun painted with his face. I'd expected shining steel or something along those lines from a god of light, but Ireland and France's faerie infestation had probably been the worst and longest lasting out of any country's, so cold iron armor made sense. They wouldn't have been able to come within ten feet of him.

A wooden spear, seven feet long and topped with a jagged, iron tip, appeared in his right hand. It then tried to leap out of his grip and impale me of its own will. Lugh was of the generation of gods that just had to have semi-intelligent, bloodthirsty weapons; he just barely held the thing back.

"Come on, Lugh," I said. "You know better than this. Look at what happened the last time there was a fight in here."

"Do not try to bluff me," he said. "No one knows if that has ever occurred. Not even the Detectives. And, truthfully, I have always wondered about this Grey Man everyone goes on about. No one has seen him. For all we know, he is a myth. Now, if you stand still, I will make this brief and painless. It will be like stepping out of a set of flabby, somewhat smelly, clothes."

"Help him!" April pleaded with Bacchus.

"Oh no, no. I'm a lover, dear, not a fighter. If you'd like me to show you –"

"Really, Bacchus?" I asked. "You're hitting on her when I'm about to be killed."

"She'll need someone to comfort her when you're gone. It is but a small service I offer. Well, I say small –"

"Can't we have one conversation that doesn't involve your penis?" I asked. "Please? I swear if I have to hear about or see one more supernatural thing's...thing tonight, I'm going to scream. And it's not exactly the thought I want to go out on."

Not that I had any intention of going out at that moment. I mainly wanted to give Lugh a chance to think over what he was doing and, hopefully, change his mind. Not that I realistically expected him to. Once an anal-retentive god like Lugh made up his mind, there's no force on the planet, common sense and logic included, that can change it.

Lugh swung his spear at me. April screamed. I just stood there, waiting.

A hand appeared on the shaft of the spear from my left, stopping it dead in its arc. The hand had a grey, almost ashy, pall to it, as if its owner had died some time back, but its skin had a suppleness that only living flesh possesses.

"No," the owner of the hand said in a soft voice that still managed to rattle my bones with its intensity.

I couldn't tell if the Grey Man really was a man. His-her-its high cheekbones and soft, smooth face made me think he was a woman, but the angles of his grey face and his somewhat broad shoulders made me think he was a man. His clothes, a three-piece charcoal suit of all lines and no curves, didn't help matters.

"Man or woman?" I asked April.

"How should I know?"

I shrugged. "That sort of thing seems more up your alley than mine."

"I don't know. Why don't you ask?"

I thought about it but then opted for a more neutral, "You guys are starting to make me feel underdressed."

"There shall be no conflict here," the Grey Man said, ignoring me. "Conflict requires division. There shall be balance, here at least."

"It's an omphalos!" April almost squealed.

"The spear?" I asked, genuinely confused as to just what the hell she was talking about.

"No, that." She pointed at the building's supporting pillar.

I looked at it, then back at the Grey Man. "I can't believe I never saw that before. She's right, isn't she?"

The Grey Man nodded, ignoring Lugh, who was trying to pull his spear from the Grey Man's hand. It wouldn't budge.

"Really?" Bacchus asked. Then he looked at the pillar and laughed. "Zeus's…," he glanced at me, "beard. I'm an idiot for not seeing that. Smart girl you've got there, Roger."

"Yeah, she is," I admitted.

"Don't sound so surprised," April said.

"Oh, I'm not. I bet you've got all kinds of hidden depths to you."

"Release Gae Assail, Border-Strider, and step outside of your domain," Lugh said, finally getting tired of trying to yank his spear away from the Grey Man. "There I will show you my power."

The Grey Man looked at Lugh with his pale eyes and the god disappeared.

"That was…impressive, actually," I said. "You need to teach me that trick."

His only response was to look at me.

"Uh, anyway, where did you send him?"

"Away. He will return at dusk on the city's border."

"He won't be happy," Bacchus said.

"We'll deal with that if it comes up," I said. "For now, you and I need to have a little talk."

"Thanks for…," I started to say to the Grey Man, but he was gone.

"You have any idea who he is?" I asked Bacchus.

100

"None," he said happily. "Marvelous to have a few mysteries left, isn't it?"

"Yeah. Marvelous."

I've never been a fan of mysteries in my city. Every mystery that I've encountered has cost me something. If I'm lucky, it only costs me a good night's sleep. Usually, though, it winds up being something a little more precious, like a girlfriend, a bit of my sanity, and once, the soul of an old friend. And now that I knew more about this particular mystery, it only made me even less of a fan. Call me crazy, but unknown, omnipotent beings in my backyard isn't my idea of a good time.

I made a mental note to check into the Grey Man after Damballa was taken care of.

"All right," I said to Bacchus. "Which room do you want to go to?"

He laughed. "Do you really need to ask?"

        *            *            *            *

"What the hell's going on?" I asked Bacchus, shifting my weight to get as comfortable as I could on one of the rough-hewn logs that served as chairs in the room.

Bacchus's favorite room also happened to be one of the oldest, as far as I could tell. Ash trees as big around as small cars formed a circle around a thick, darkly stained, deeply gouged wooden table, blocking out most of the Warren's light. A gently crackling fire glowed just to my right from a pit dug deeply into the soil serving as the room's floor. The rich smell of damp earth filled the air, along with the occasional wolf howl from somewhere close.

I'd never liked this room. It smelled too much of earth and all of the old, bloody rituals used to encourage things to grow. Too many of the blackened gouges on the table came in evenly spread fours for my comfort, too much life came from the trees. I didn't sense any ghosts, but there was something, just on the edge of my senses.

"Do you mind?" Bacchus asked from the other side of the table, going to remove his suit's jacket.

"Just leave the pants on," I said.

"Thanks."

He sighed as he removed his jacket. "Why you people feel the need to wrap yourselves in so much clothing is beyond me."

"Beats me."

"It's like you're trying to put on some kind armor against the world," he continued, loosening his tie. "Maybe if you had more hair…"

"Well, in my defense, I like having pockets. And it gets damn cold around here in the winter."

"And I definitely don't want to see him naked," April said, wrinkling her nose.

"Thanks," I said. "That's the one thing this night was missing for me: getting shot down by a dead stripper."

Bacchus laughed. "Oh, give her a break, Roger. She's just doing what your culture has told her to. And you aren't an attractive man."

"Yeah, yeah, our culture sucks, but it's all we've got. And I'd like to keep it around, so how about you tell me what you know."

He began to unbutton his shirt, revealing a chest and shoulders covered in a pelt of curly, black hair.

"The man of two worlds, the woman of two lives, and the child of two skins will bridge the way to the first Hell."

"That's it?" I asked.

"It sounds better in Greek," Bacchus admitted. "But it's pretty clear for a prophecy. You, some woman, and a kid are going to help open up Hell."

"Is Beth the woman?" April asked. "I mean, she's reincarnated, so she's had two lives."

"Technically, we all are," I said. "But you're probably right. Good job."

She smiled. "Was that a compliment?"

"Don't get used to it."

"Be nice, boy," Bacchus said.

"Thank you," April said. "He's been doing that all night."

"It's been a rough day, all right?" I sighed. "I suppose you heard about Vesta."

"She talked to me before she saw you, yes. I offered to console her, of course, but she politely refused."

"What? A virgin goddess refusing you? I'm shocked."

"I wanted her to go out with a bang," he said with a wink.

April groaned.

"Stop it," I told him.

"My point is, Roger, that she knew exactly what she was doing. She was the best of us. The Romans knew that. You should feel honored that she trusted you enough to come to you to help her."

"Aww," April said. "She liked you."

I glared at her. "I know. But it's still a shitty thing."

Bacchus reached across the table and clapped me on the shoulder. "When this is over, I'll take you out for a night of drinking you'll never remember."

I smiled. "You're on."

"So," I said, "Damballa's going to use Beth, me, and I'm guessing the reincarnated naga to open a gate to the first Hell. Any idea what that is?"

He shrugged. "Bad?"

I narrowed my eyes. "Thanks."

He laughed. "What do you want from me? If you want to get drunk, grow grapes, or go mad, then you come to me. I don't worry about the afterlife."

I knew this was a lie, but I got his point. Bacchus had harrowed the Underworld a few times in the past, but, to him, that wasn't much more than a trip to Detroit would be for me. Probably less dangerous.

"What about the nagas, then?" I asked. "Why is Damballa working with them to bring Hell on Earth?"

"Who knows? That snake's slithered around forever. Longer than me, anyway. Might be he made some deal with them from the old days."

"How old?"

Bacchus smiled, revealing teeth stained a dark yellow-brown, possibly from wine, but probably not. "The days when gods were things, not people. Primal forces, like Night, Sun, Rock."

"People worshipped rocks?" April asked.

"People still worship rocks," I said off-handedly. Then, to Bacchus, "Snake?"

He nodded.

"So, he's a primal force in human clothes."

"Maybe. But here's something even more awful to chew on: what if he's something worse that we've never seen before?"

"There's something worse?"

The only primal force that I'd ever had to deal with was Rain during the War of Storms, and then I'd had just about every god, spirit, and notion even remotely connected to water helping me. Granted, Rain was one of the stronger primals, but still, I didn't even want to think about something that could be worse.

"Have you ever heard a naga swear?" Bacchus asked.

I thought about it. "I really don't know. I've heard them talk in their own language, but I'll be damned if I know what they're saying. One did mention a place called Sraatsa earlier tonight, though, now that you mention it."

"I've heard them. They swear just like me and you, calling on gods."

"I'm going to stop you right there. There's no way that Damballa is one of their gods. No one knows when they all died out, but there had to have been thousands, hell, probably millions of years between that and humans coming onto the scene. No god can go that long living on the belief of a few ghosts."

"I hope you're right, Roger."

I slapped the table to break the mood. "On that cheery note, I've got the body of a stripper in my trunk that needs disposing of. No need to cart it around all night."

Bacchus stood up, shaking his head. "I can't let you go out, Roger. I'm sorry. You can stay here, and I'll buy you whatever you want. I'll even get some of the ladies from this little place I know down the road to make a house-call. We'll make a night of it."

"What about the Grey Man?" April asked.

"The Grey Man probably can't touch him," I said. "Though I'm not sure I'd bet on it like Bacchus is."

A wooden staff topped with a pine cone appeared in Bacchus's left hand. "I am the god of madness. The god of outsiders. The god of the wild night."

"A god of chaos with too big a sense of self-importance," I finished. "A god who's going to have to come through this table to get me."

Bacchus laughed. "This little thing?"

He reached down with one hand, ripped the table from the ground and tossed it aside.

"Easily done. I only look like a fat man, Roger. You'd do well to remember that."

I smiled in that worrying way of mine that Bacchus knew all too well. It was an expression that meant I'd just conned whoever was after me into setting themselves up. And then he sensed it, the massive build-up of spiritual pressure in the trees as hundreds of spirits noticed that, after hundreds, maybe thousands, of years, the lock on their cage has been ripped off.

April ran, not even bothering to ask what was going on.

"What did you do?" Bacchus asked.

"Me?" I said, rubbing my temples to help with the headache all of those ghosts manifesting at once was starting to give me. "You're the idiot who let them out."

I didn't know for sure that the table was holding them in, but it seemed like a safe bet. The person is sacrificed, his soul is sucked down through the table and into the trees, whose roots were probably twisted around the table's legs. Efficient system. Horrific on several levels, but efficient.

"You're the idiot that goaded me into it!"

The room started shaking. Support beams groaned in outrage from somewhere.

"This is how you want to go? Arguing about blame?"

"It will take more than a few spirits to end me, boy."

"You're a god of life, Bacchus. These things will tear you apart. And it feels like there are more than enough pissed off dead people here to take you out permanently."

Something cracked loudly and the room slanted to the left.

"Leave me alone and I'll fix this," I said, trying to keep my balance.

"This is going to take more than one of those foul cigars of yours, Roger."

"Quit stalling."

Half of the trees exploded down their middles, popping like the world's largest string of firecrackers and sending splinters shooting at us, cutting my left cheek in two, shallow slashes. Blue light boiled out of the cracks. The remaining trees whumphed into conflagrations of blue flames, sucking all of the heat out of the room to fuel themselves.

"I figure we've got about a minute until they rush out of those trees and rip our...my soul and your essence apart," I said, my breath appearing in little puffs of fog.

"Oh fine."

"Swear by the Styx."

For the Greek gods, swearing by the River Styx is an unbreakable vow. Most pantheons had vows like that, gods being notorious for reneging on their promises, even to each other. Demons kept their word more often than your average god.

"What?" he asked.

Dozens of spectral arms reached out of the ground where the table had been rooted.

105

That seemed to convince him. "I swear by the Styx that I'll leave you alone. Now do something!"

I swung a fist a Bacchus. Just before it connected, an ashy hand as cool and smooth as marble caught it.

"Send this room to the Asylum Tower!" I shouted at the Grey Man.

No emotions registered on his face.

Bodies began to pull themselves out of the trees like some awful blossoming. Each one had a large, bloody hole in the same spot in its chest. Each one's eyes rolled in its head like a mad bull's. And each one let loose a scream that set my soul to vibrating.

"They're going to try to kill us," I prompted.

The ground began crumbling and little blue flames popped up all around us. The screams crescendoed into something that threatened to shatter my spirit like a wine glass at a diva convention.

"I cannot send the room there. It is another's domain."

"The nearest intersection, then," I said. "Howard and Oakland."

Bacchus started dancing around as hands shot out of the ground and tried to latch onto his feet.

And then we were all standing on the main floor, April included, near the Warren's side entrance. My stomach lurched at the sudden change in position, and I had to squint at the bright light, but otherwise everything seemed to be in one piece.

"You got them there?" I asked the Grey Man.

"Yes."

"Good. The Tower should suck them up. After all those years trapped in that room and those trees, they should qualify as crazy enough to get in."

"You must leave," the Grey Man said to me. "There shall be no conflict here. You may return in a week."

"Not a problem," I said and walked to the door.

"No hard feelings?" Bacchus asked, following me.

"You were just trying to protect me. And I appreciate that, but I've got a job to do. Just so we're clear, though, if you ever do that again I'm going to tell the cops about Lisa. You won't be able to show that face in town for twenty years." Gods of debauchery and statutory rape laws never go well together.

His face turned so red I couldn't tell if he was embarrassed or angry. "How is it my fault that –"

I held up a hand. "Save it. If you'll excuse me, I have a body to get rid of."

Still flushed, Bacchus offered me his hand. "Good luck, Roger."

I took it and he pulled me into a hairy bear hug that smelled vaguely of grape juice.

"Don't get killed," he said after he released me.

"I'll do my best."

April managed to stay quiet until we got to the Sunbird. "I'm sorry I ran away."

"You did the only smart thing," I told her over the car's roof. "Hell, if I could've run I would've."

"So you're not mad?"

"No. Now, if you ask me that question after I have to manhandle your body into a grave, you might get a different answer."

She gave me a genuine smile. As we started toward the cemetery, I had to wonder if it was the first honest thing I'd gotten from her.

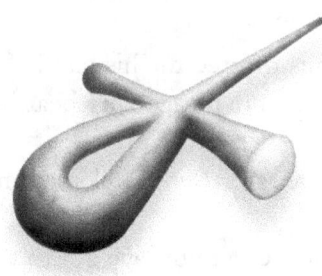

## 6.

"I love cemeteries," I said after tossing April's earthly remains onto the muddy, freshly filled grave of Elizabeth Williamson, 1898-1997, 1998-2000, 2001-2002 May She Find Peace At Last [7]. I wiped my hands on my coat. "They're always so quiet, especially this late at night. No people, no ghosts, no gods, no nothing."

We started walking down one of the paths, back to the Sunbird.

"I was always afraid of cemeteries when I was alive," April said, slightly embarrassed. "I thought they were haunted."

I gave a short laugh. "What ghost in its right, or even wrong, mind wants to hang about in a cemetery? Especially one like this."

"You just said you love cemeteries."

"I do, but that doesn't make this one any less creepy," I said, looking around at the gravestone covered hills. "It's just too…rolling to be a cemetery."

"So you're saying you're prejudiced toward hilly cemeteries."

"Just this one."

April looked back over her shoulder. "There is one other bad thing about cemeteries."

"What's that?"

A pair of headlights came on behind us, followed quickly by blue and red flashing lights and a siren chirp.

I dropped my head and put my hands up. "Damned cops."

"Put your hands on your head and turn around slowly," a young man's voice said through a speaker. I didn't recognize it.

I did as I was told.

---

[7] You ever wish Grandma was still around for Christmas? Betty Williamson was a good example of why you should just get over it, especially if you're descended from necromancers.

A police officer stepped out of the black cruiser and approached me, making sure to keep his right hand on his holstered pistol. He had a young, eager face that looked like it only needed a shave every other week. His uniform even still had its pleats.

"Step over to the front of my car and put your hands on the hood, please, sir," he said with only a hint of shakiness.

"You're new, aren't you?" I asked as I walked to his car. I looked down and read the man's name-tag. "Officer Hendricks. And don't worry, there's nothing in my coat that'll poke you."

Officer Hendricks began patting me down. "You seem to know the routine pretty well. Do you get arrested often, sir?"

"Not anymore. What am I being arrested for?"

"Do you realize that you're trespassing?"

Fortunately, I'd had enough foresight to put my gun in the Sunbird's glove compartment, so, other than a small pocketknife that smelled vaguely of urinal cakes and a small, thin bone that may or may not have been human, there was nothing potentially awkward to be found on me. Officer Hendricks held on to the pocketknife after removing it from my pocket, giving me further indication as to where the next few hours of my evening were going to be spent.

"It was the only time I had free on my calendar," I said casually after he was through.

"You wouldn't happen to know anything about the body lying back there, would you sir?"

*Shit*, I swore mentally.

I tried to look surprised. "There's a body?"

"Yes, sir. And since you're the only one around, I'm afraid that I'm going to have to ask you to come along with me." Officer Hendricks reached for his cuffs.

"I don't suppose me telling you that you're making a horrible mistake will help?" I tried.

"No, sir," he said flatly.

I sighed. "That's what I thought."

I knew the drill well enough to not resist. Soon, I was sitting, handcuffed, on a hard, fiberglass seat in the back of the cruiser and on my way downtown, swearing to myself the whole way. Naturally, April accompanied me.

\*   \*   \*   \*

The concrete cell I'd been tossed in was filled with the stench of ammonia, urine, and vomit. Despite my request for an empty cell, it was also filled with people of various sizes, shapes, and degrees of cleanliness, each wearing the same prison orange I'd been forced into. Luckily, none of them recognized me.

"I liked it when you told him that you didn't want a free call because it was past his mom's bedtime," April teased.

"Every cop knows that I get my own cell when I'm here," I said quietly behind my hand as I faked rubbing my nose. "It makes my stay a lot easier on them."

"Why's that?"

"Because I usually have a 'guest' with me. And looking like I'm talking to myself upsets some of the more…eccentric inmates."

I scanned the blue cell for ghosts. Seeing none, I relaxed a bit. "At least Bob's not here," I whispered.

"Who?"

"An old friend from my Ace days. He likes to hang out in jail for some reason."

"Why does —"

I held up my hand to stop any more questions. "Shush. In jail."

After about ten minutes, an older, balding officer with a slight paunch came to the cell. "Roger Freeman," he called out. Freeman wasn't my real last name, but it was good enough for all of the IDs I had on me.

I stepped up to the bars. "That's me."

"You're being moved to your own cell." He unlocked the door. "Follow me, please."

"'Bout damn time," I said under my breath as I left.

When we were out of sight of the other inmates, I asked, "How's it going, Tim? It's been a while."

Tim shrugged. "Can't complain. Wife's still getting on me about working nights. She thinks I should try and get on first shift so we can spend our nights together."

"Which is exactly why you work third shift."

"Right." He unlocked a small cell and I walked in. It was closed behind me.

"Get Carlson in here as soon as you can, Tim," I said with all seriousness. "Things are pretty bad tonight."

"I'll try, but he's started turning the ringer off on his phone this late at night."

"Dammit, I need out."

Tim had been working with the Kalamazoo police long enough to know that I rarely did anything illegal without good cause. He didn't always understand the exact reasoning behind what I did, but he'd heard a few of the stories and believed enough of them to not ask questions.

"I'll send a cruiser over to wake him up. You owe me one, Roger."

"Yeah, yeah. If we're still all here tomorrow, we'll work something out. And bring me my clothes. I hate these prison issue things."

"Do you want a mint for your pillow, too?"

"If you've got one."

Tim walked away, shaking his head.

"So what's going on now, Ace?" a man's voice said from behind me.

"As if this night wasn't bad enough," I said as I turned around. "And stop calling me Ace, Bob. Nobody's called me that in eight years."

The man standing at the back of my cell could best be described as five-by-five. In life, Bob had been a sphere of flesh too lazy to move out of his parents' house until it collapsed on him. A kind of friend from high school, his death during the War of Storms was my fault, and it was the only reason I didn't toss his soul in a urinal cake and forget about it.

April instinctually moved closer to me.

"Sorry, Ace. Old habits are hard to break." Bob looked over to April and leered. "You're doing okay for yourself. She's hot."

"Bob, shut up. I'm not that desperate for a woman yet."

"Who is this?" April asked from over my shoulder.

"This is my old friend, for lack of a better word, Bob. If you looked up 'moral turpitude' in the dictionary, you'd see his picture. He'd sell his grandmother for the right price. Other than that, he's an idiot but not too horrible of a guy."

"She was worth $18.20, back then," Bob said. "I bet I could get more for her now, though."

"She's dead, Bob."

"So?"

"You're sick. You know that, don't you," I said.

"Can't be sick. I'm dead."

I went to the cell's small cot and sat down, refusing to be his straight man for the evening. April followed closely.

"Hey Ace, did you tell her about Delilah yet?" Bob asked.

"Why the hell would I tell her about Delilah?" I said, knowing full well that I was going to have to tell April the story. "And don't call me Ace."

"He used to date the Antichrist," Bob told April.

"I thought you were straight," April said to me.

"I am. The Antichrist's a woman named Delilah. And she's not really the Antichrist. There's no such thing. She's just Jesus's cousin, or half-sister, or whatever. It's hard to describe with that family. We still talk sometimes."

"It was funny. The Antichrist dating the Antichrist," Bob said.

"I never did get to put you in a urinal cake for calling me the Antichrist, Bob," I told him. "Just be happy I don't have my pocketknife."

"Why did he call you that?" April asked.

"Because I became an atheist and started having severe problems with hard-core religious people back when I was twenty. Seeing the occasional ghost will do that to a person. So Bob started calling me the Antichrist, and it got abbreviated to Ace after a while. Took me three years to get people to stop calling me that."

"How'd you meet the real Antichrist?"

"That's a pretty long story," I lied, trying not to have to tell it. It wasn't that it was painful or anything as much as it reminded me of a few regrets that I preferred not to think about.

"We've got time, Ace," Bob said. "Or I can tell it."

"No," I said quickly. "But I will tell you why she left me."

I rubbed my eyes. "I could be using this time to sleep."

I thought for a moment about where to begin. "This was back before I started seeing ghosts on a regular basis. I could occasionally see them, but not like I can now. It was kind of like having a TV station in my head, but the reception went in and out. And I sure as hell hadn't run into any gods."

*     *     *     *

February 24, 1995. Funny how some dates just stick out in your memory. That's the day the city screwed me over. Delilah and I had decided to walk from my apartment to the walking mall downtown, back before the city decided to put a road through it in an effort to increase business. A cold wind would whip up occasionally, throwing snow and ice particles in our mostly numb faces and causing Delilah's long, thick, coppery hair to flow out behind her. It was still one of my favorite images of her. Aside from her naked, of course, but that kind of went without saying.

It was around noon, but the winter sun just made the snow on the ground blinding and did little to make anyone warm. A sunny day in February was pretty rare, though, so I didn't see the need to complain.

We'd made it as far as Bronson Park when the hairs on the back of my neck stood on end, and not from the cold. I recognized the sensation from the few times over the years that I'd encountered ghosts, so I stopped and turned to face the spirit. Delilah turned, too.

A short, bald man in a trench coat stood there, his hands shoved deep in his pockets like the cold actually bothered him. Thinking about it later, I figured he did that to make the whole scene seem as normal as possible. Of course, normally, little clouds of breath would have occasionally puffed out from his bulbous nose, and snowflakes wouldn't have whizzed right through him.

"What?" I asked it.

"Oh you'll be great at this," the dead man said. "Relax, kid. I'm here to give you a job."

This was a new experience for me. Usually ghosts just acted creepy or angry about being dead when I ran into them. They'd never shown up with job opportunities.

"What if I don't want it?" I asked, suspicious of anyone, especially a dead guy, giving me anything.

Delilah looked hard at the ghost. "Tony? Is that you?"

Tony smiled. "Yeah, it's me. Heart attack. I guess smoking really can punch your ticket."

I looked at her. "You can see ghosts, too?"

"She's Ashera's daughter," he said. "What do you think?"

"Why didn't you tell me?" I asked, ignoring the ghost for the moment.

Delilah shrugged. "It never came up."

Like any relationship, ours had certain phrases that meant shut up, or stop asking, or you're about to do something that will piss me off to no end. "It never came up" was one of them that Delilah used. Generally, it meant "I'm a semi-divine being who's trying not to freak you out with all of the weird shit that comes along with that." So I dropped it and turned back to Tony.

"How do you know who she is?"

113

"It's my job. Or was until about ten minutes ago. I was the city's Detective."

Delilah's eyes widened. "No! He's not going to do it, Tony. You can't make him."

Tony motioned for her to stop. "First off, I'm not picking him, the city is. If it were up to me, nobody'd be doing this. I'm just playing Jacob Marley in this drama and warning him of the ghosts to come. Secondly, he doesn't have a choice."

Confused as to exactly what I was being picked for, but pretty sure it was about as good as being picked to tell Hitler his ideas were a little extreme, I asked, "What the hell are you two talking about? Picked for what?"

Tony smiled sadly. "Congratulations, kid. You've been chosen by the powers that be, mainly be dicks, to be Kalamazoo's new Detective, effective immediately. Any psychic abilities you have are now fully up and running. Your office is over there," Tony pointed vaguely northeast. "Delilah will show you where. And your life is now officially gone. Have fun. Don't kick out the poltergeist."

"What?" I asked.

"Ah, the tradition of excellence continues. I reacted the same way." Tony's tone became serious. "Can the poltergeist stay in the office?"

This last part seemed especially important to the ghost, so I agreed to it with a nod, too confused to really say much of anything else.

Tony clapped his hands and rubbed them together. "Great. They key's under the mat, my body's lying on the floor of the office near the bathroom. Officer Carlson knows what to do with it. Have fun."

Tony then spread his arms wide and melodramatically said, "Hark! A great, white light. I think I shall go into it."

He disappeared.

"Tony, you ass, get back here!" Delilah shouted loudly enough for half of the people in the park to stop and stare at her.

"Fuck," she muttered.

"What just happened?" I asked.

"I hate this town," Delilah grumbled as she started walking across the park. "I knew I should've gotten you to move."

I followed her. "Delilah, tell me what's going on."

She did, at least what she knew. Not even a month later, we'd broken up.

\*          \*          \*          \*

"That's awful!" April said.

"Try living it," I growled.

"It is a pretty messed up story," Bob said, sitting on the floor. "If I hadn't met Delilah, I wouldn't even believe it."

"That and the whole being a ghost thing," I reminded him.

"Yeah, and that. Dude, she was hot, too. You shouldn't have broken up with her."

"She broke up with me, Bob," I shouted. "You think I didn't want to stay with her?"

"You're sounding all bitter again, Ace," Bob said.

"Yeah," April agreed. "Calm down a bit."

"Screw you both," I said angrily. "You're dead, so your problems with the world are just about nil. I never even got to graduate from college. This job more or less saw to that."

"So why are you still around?" April asked Bob, ignoring me as I ranted.

"I don't know. Just didn't feel like leaving."

"I'll tell you why," I said. "See, there are three basic kinds of ghosts: ones that are here because they don't know they're dead, ones with unfinished business, and ones that don't want to move on for some reason. You're in the unfinished business category," I nodded to April. "Fat boy here was just too lazy to move on. He saw the light, walked toward it, and decided he needed a nap."

"So where is Delilah now?" April asked, ignoring what I'd just said.

I thought for a moment. "Last time I heard, she was hanging out with some guy in Orlando. But that was about two years ago, so she could be anywhere by now."

"Want me to find her for you?" Bob asked.

I narrowed my eyes. "That would involve a lot of walking, Bob. Why do you want to do that?"

He shrugged. "I just figured that maybe she could help with this whole Hell-on-Earth thing that's going on."

My mind stopped for a second. Finally, I managed, "What Hell-on-Earth thing, Bob?"

"The one the nagas are doing. Y'know, getting all of the nagas out of naga Hell."

"You are so going into a urinal cake you dead, fat bastard," I said evenly. "Why in the name of every god in this town didn't you tell me about this sooner?"

"Dude, no offense, but your apartment stinks. I'm not going in there unless I have to."

I stood up and started pacing, running a hand through my hair. "The end of the world didn't seem important enough?"

Bob, finally realizing he'd screwed up big, stood up and started inching his way toward a wall. "I'm dead, Ace. The end of the world doesn't mean much to me, man."

I stopped pacing and glared at him. Through clenched teeth, I said, "Go. Find. Delilah. Or I feed you to the Evil House. Slowly."

Bob ran through the wall.

I went over to the spot on the wall Bob had passed through and kicked it until my foot hurt. Then I used the other foot.

"I hate dead people," I finally said to the universe in general.

"Except for me," April supplied hopefully.

"No, I pretty much hate you, too. I'm in that non-specific rage phase of tiredness and frustration currently. If you're dead, I'm not too pleased with you."

I sat back down on the cot. "Screw it. I'm taking a nap. Don't bother me."

I'd just laid down when I heard a resonant man's voice say, "That better not include me, Roger, after having one of my men wake me up at one in the morning."

I groaned. "At least you've gotten some sleep, Carlson," I said, not getting up.

"That's your fault, from what I'm hearing. What did you do to that poor girl's body?"

I decided it would be best to at least be polite to the man I'd woken up this late, so I sat up. "Shot it several times after it chased me down and killed a guy. It's lucky I didn't put it in a septic tank to rot."

Carlson, middle aged with the slight paunch and greying hair to prove it, took out his keys and used one to open my cell door. He'd probably just gotten up, but you couldn't tell it by looking at him. Clean-shaven, neatly dressed in a dark blue, button-up shirt and matching tie, he had a vigor to him that belied the early hour. I'd always kind of wondered if Carlson was human or something else, but I didn't have the heart to ask him. We've all got our secrets, after all.

"Anything I should know about?" he asked.

I stood up. Carlson knew a surprising amount of what was going on in his town, I'd found out over the years. I'd also learned to play pretty straight with the man. "Not unless you know how to keep the ghosts of seven-foot-tall lizard people from somehow opening a gate to Hell."

"Can't say I do."

"Didn't think so. My advice to you on this whole matter, then, is to go home and tell your wife you love her like it was the last time. Because it might be."

"That bad?" Carlson asked.

"Remember the time we found Jormangandr in the sewers?"

"Yeah," Carlson said slowly.

"That's fun compared to this."

"Who's that?" April asked.

"Big Viking serpent-thing. Kills Thor on Viking doomsday," I said quickly. "Focus."

"Friend in there with you?" Carlson asked.

"The ghost that used to own the body I shot up. I'll tell you the story later, hopefully. Can I go save the world now?"

Carlson stepped out of the doorway. "Be my guest. But you owe me for waking me up. And, I'm assuming, for blocking an intersection with a small forest."

"Yeah, yeah. Get in line," I said as I walked out of the cell. "I'm tempted to let the world end just so I don't have to pay back all of the favors I'm going to owe after tonight."

"Who do you owe?" Carlson asked, escorting me out of the cell block.

"Mama Rosa."

He grinned. "You must have been desperate to need a favor from her."

I shrugged. "It's not too bad. I just have to take Beth out on a date."

Carlson raised an eyebrow. "The Beth whose body she's in? You do know what a date with that woman would involve, don't you?"

"Aside from possibly the weirdest ménage a trois in existence?"

"Maybe, but it can't be any freakier than me and the Fates."

"Even the old one?" I asked, moderately frightened of the answer. Though, I had to admit, he went up a little in my esteem if that adventure

117

was anywhere near true.

"It's sort of a package deal with them," Carlson said. "It was back in my young days, before I met Brianna. I'll tell you about it someday."

I smiled. "Can't wait. I never thought you to be the wild and crazy type, Carlson."

The chief chuckled. "You'd be surprised some of the things your predecessor and I did."

"Yeah, well, he was in a pretty big hurry to move on when he finally got the chance, so he didn't tell me a whole lot about his past."

Carlson stopped at the door to the storage room for prisoners' clothes and possessions. "Tony was a good guy, Roger. You would've liked him."

"I keep hearing that. Someday I'll have to get Mama Rosa to try and contact him and see what he didn't tell me."

"You should. Meanwhile, let's get you dressed and out of here. I want to wake up alive tomorrow."

After I'd gotten changed and repocketed all of my paraphernalia, I put out my hand, and Carlson shook it. "I had your car towed here when I heard you'd been arrested. I'll make sure to hide the fact that we found Miss Goode's purse in it, by the way. You're getting sloppy, Roger."

"Damn," I swore loudly and stomped on the floor with my left foot, causing it to throb some from the earlier kicking I'd given the wall. "Thanks. I owe you another one. I was going to drop it off at my place, but I guess I forgot."

"It's all right. You're tired. Just make sure you save the world, huh?"

"I'll do my best."

"And you said something about someone getting killed?"

"Yeah." I told him where the naga had shot the guy with a fatal case of curious. "I'd be pretty surprised if no one called it in, considering all the noise we made."

"I'll send someone over, just in case. Good luck, Roger."

"Thanks. I'm probably going to need it."

*　　　*　　　*　　　*

"Why did he let you out?" April asked once we were back on the road.

"Carlson's a good guy," I replied. "He knows what's really going on in this town. And I got his mother's ghost to tell me where she hid the key to her safety deposit box."

"So, where to now?" April asked.

"Back to my apartment for another urinal cake and some supplies. Then I'm going to talk to Samedi again. Along the way I'll decide if I should kill his drunk ass for helping this thing along."

We made it a few blocks to Lovell Street, a couple blocks down from the Evil House, where a large group of nagas walked into the street, forcing us to stop. They all wore scaled, leather armor of some kind, sutured together from the remains of gods only knew what kind of animals. Severed claws the size of daggers and horns longer than my arm jutted out from their armor's shoulders, spines, and elbows. A few even carried jagged bone swords, which was new. I'd never seen nagas manifest armor or weaponry of any kind. It made sense, I guess. They'd had a civilization of some kind, after all. Still, when ancient evil spirits do something new, it's time to start worrying.

Then the full impact of what was going on registered in my tired mind.

"This is bad," I said slowly. "They've never gotten together like that before. They must be doing their ritual somewhere around here."

I looked in my rearview and started backing up, but stopped when another group of nagas, dressed the same as the others, walked out of the parking lot of an apartment complex and faced us.

"Looks like they're all here," I said.

"What're we going to do?" April said, terrified.

"Play a game of chicken."

I revved the Sunbird's engine a couple of times.

The nagas in front of us, understanding what I was doing, crouched down, getting ready to charge.

"I really hope this works," I said.

April's eyes shot back and forth between me and the nagas in front of us. "Hope what works?"

I punched it, the tires squawking some.

The nagas screamed something impossible for humans to repeat and ran at us, weapons raised.

April screamed as I crashed right into them, sending their weightless bodies flying in all directions. I kept going, running two lights in the process, and didn't stop until we were a mile or so away.

"Stupid things," I said, smiling.

"What just happened?" April asked, positive that she should be dead again.

"Do you know what a ward is?"

April shook her head.

"It's like a force field that keeps out ghosts. Papa Legba put one on my car a while back. They're easy to get through if you know how, but we were moving fast, so I figured it was worth risking. Still, dressed up like that, if they'd managed to get through we would've been dead, I don't care what Damballa says about them not being allowed to kill me."

"I'm already dead. How can they kill me again?"

"Don't worry about it. Let's just get what I need and get this night over with."

"When do you think Bob will get back with Delilah?" April asked after we'd been driving for a minute.

"Never. He's probably either forgotten what he's doing or lost. I just did it to get rid of him before I started thinking of ways to send him to Hell. Aside from Beth, we're pretty much on our own."

"Oh."

The rest of the mercifully short drive was spent in silence.

\*         \*         \*         \*

When we pulled into my parking spot, I told April, "Stay here. I'll only be a minute."

"Not a problem. Bob's right, that place stinks."

"Yeah, yeah," I said as I got out of the Sunbird.

Once inside, I made sure to turn on the light to keep from tripping, falling, and killing myself on a pile of something. I ran to my bathroom, a meticulously clean contradiction to the rest of my apartment that I scrubbed down at least twice a week to keep out anything that might try and wander in from the living room. When it came to a choice between ghosts and bathroom borne diseases, I always chose ghosts. At any rate, not that many thought to appear there.

I grabbed a pair of pre-carved urinal cakes and a large, silver ankh out of the medicine cabinet. Yes, a medicine cabinet was a strange place to put about five pounds of silver, but storing it there kept it away from most of the supernatural things that popped into, broke into, or crashed into my apartment. Most of them wouldn't be able to come near it anyway, but it never hurt to be careful. Silver, I learned pretty early on, is the best thing in the world for taking out evil supernatural critters. It has a mystical purity to it that no other metal has. Don't ask me why because I've never found out. Problem is, it usually gets a bit corrupted when it comes into contact with them and eventually becomes useless. Hence keeping it in the bathroom. The ankh shape, as a symbol of life, made it just about invincible for beating back dead things and gods of death. Put the two together and it made a hell of a weapon for someone in my line of work.

Next, I went to the living room and dug out the phone from underneath a pile of old pizza boxes. I dialed Beth's number, growing more impatient with each ring. After four of them, the voice mail picked up, and Beth's voice said, "I'm not in, leave a message. Unless this is Roger, in which case we know, and you need to get a move on it. They've probably got me by now and are just about ready." Then a beep.

I hung up the phone. "Damn."

I calmed myself for a moment, not wanting April to see how upset I was, and then walked out to the Sunbird.

"Get everything?" April asked when I'd gotten in the car. She scooted away from me some, almost unnoticeably.

"Yeah. We've got another stop to make before we go see Samedi, though."

"Where?"

"Beth's place. I think we've got a meeting set up."

"With Beth, or with Mama Rosa?"

"Neither," I said and left it at that.

*      *      *      *

I will say that the trap the nagas had set for me looked pretty good from the outside. They'd left Beth's living room light on to make it seem like she was still there, and the only car in the driveway was hers. The kid must have parked whatever he'd driven there some ways down the street, or maybe even in the parking lot of the convenience store at the end of the street. I could probably work out which one it was if I'd really wanted to, but didn't see the need. I couldn't sense any ghosts nearby, but that didn't really mean much if they were hiding in the kid's body. The front door, open a crack, spoiled the set up a bit, but not much. I might have even fallen for it if I hadn't called first.

"Stay here. I've got a trap to walk into," I said.

April asked the logical question, "Why are you walking into a trap? That's kind of stupid, isn't it?"

"Not if I know it's a trap," I said as I got out of the car. "Hopefully I can get some information out of this."

I walked up to the door and knocked on it.

It opened all the way, revealing the kid from earlier that evening.

"Hope I didn't keep you waiting too long," I told him.

"Nope. You're right on time. Come on in." The kid stepped back to let me in.

I walked in and the kid shut the door behind me.

"You know we're going to kill you, right?" the kid asked me.

It looked like somebody hadn't gotten Damballa's message to leave me alive.

"I know you're going to try, but I really doubt you'll do it, kid," I said as I walked into the kitchen and started opening cupboards.

"Don't call me kid. My name's Charles Jones."

"Hey, kid," I shouted back into the living room, "she didn't happen to tell you where Mama Rosa kept her rum, did she?"

The kid came into the kitchen. "What the hell are you doing? I just said that we're going to kill you."

"And I said that I doubt it, which means I need some rum for later," I told him as calmly as my nerves would let me. I was in danger, don't get me wrong, but I wasn't about to show some kid how nervous I was, either. "Look in the refrigerator for me, would you?"

He walked up to me and began shouting. "Don't you get it? We're going to kill you, open the door to Sraatsa, and then kill off all your race. You and all of the other hairless apes on this planet will be dead. And you can't stop it."

I moved a bottle of whiskey aside in the cupboard I was looking through. "Ah, found it." I looked at him. "All of us, huh?"

"Yes," he said with a smile.

I took one of Mama Rosa's bottles of "special" rum out of the cupboard and put it in a trench coat pocket. "You, too?"

His smile flickered for an instant. "I'm not human."

"Really?" I reached out and pinched the kid. I knew this was pushing my luck, but I couldn't resist myself. "You feel human to me."

He slapped my hand away. "Only my body's human. My soul is naga."

"Was," I corrected. "Funny thing about reincarnation. Whatever you reincarnate as, your soul becomes. If I died right now and came back as a cat, my soul would be a cat's soul. An incredibly smart and attractive cat, but still a cat. Same goes for you, which makes you one hundred percent human."

"You're lying," the kid said with some uncertainty.

I began walking back to the front door. "Am I? Ask your friends in your head. They know I'm telling the truth."

I opened the door and ran to the Sunbird, leaving the kid standing there talking to himself. I managed to be in the car and driving away in less than ten seconds.

"I hate kids," I said once we were away. "But I love how stupid they are sometimes."

"He seemed pretty smart when we saw him by the fountain," April said a little defensively.

"Hey now, don't go rooting for the bad guys. The ghosts helping him are smart. He, on the other hand, is just some punk kid with delusions of grandeur who, fortunately, doesn't seem to remember his past life. I'm guessing we have Samedi to thank for that small favor."

A glance in the rearview showed me that no one was following us.

"He's been keeping us going all night," she pointed out.

"True, but that's just because I was playing catch-up. Now we go on the offensive."

*       *       *       *

"Looks like everybody's still here," I said from the driver's seat, noting all of the cars that remained parked on both roads near Ron's house, a good number of them sporting little orange ticket envelopes under their wiper blades. "Which means Samedi's still here, too."

I noticed April's eyes starting to drift in the direction of the Evil House. "How about you come with me this time? I don't want to risk the Evil House eating you while I'm gone."

"Huh?" April looked at me without really seeing.

I sighed and took out the ankh. "I should've thought of this earlier."

A small flash of light flared where I tapped her on the shoulder. She jumped like a cattle prod had just poked her.

"Ow, fuck!" she screamed. "What the hell is that?"

"A Taser for dead things," I said with a slight smile. "It's a combination of the silver and the ankh symbol. A mystically pure metal in the shape of the symbol of life are the Wonder Twins of dead-thing kryptonite."

"Next time just use the cigar," April whined, rubbing her shoulder. "That hurt."

"Yeah, well, it's close to being plutonium for gods of death like Samedi. It's a little more forceful than I usually like, but it's pretty late in the game." I put it back in a trench-coat pocket.

I got out of the Sunbird. "Let's go."

Sleeping people in various degrees of nudity were spread out everywhere we walked. The level of heat in the room had gone from tropical to just marginally uncomfortable.

"Did you walk through here with your eyes closed earlier?" April asked, smiling.

"That could have caused some problems. But, yeah, it was tough to get through here without at least staying for a quickie."

"Is that Roger I hear in there?" Samedi said from the next room.

We walked in and found him sitting on the ledge of a picture window. A pale, naked woman lay slumped against his shoulder.

Samedi smiled when he saw us. "Roger! How nice it is to see you again. Excuse me for a moment, and I'll clear you a place to sit."

He gently picked up the woman and laid her on the floor among some other partiers. "Much better. Now, please sit, and introduce me to your lovely companion."

"Far be it from me to refuse a request from Baron Samedi." I sat next to him.

Samedi laughed. "I know that tone. You're wanting something from me."

"Yeah, and it's something pretty big. But first, this is my client, April. She was murdered by the naga you reincarnated."

Samedi nodded to April, who had remained standing. "My apologies, my dear. If I had known that so beautiful of a woman would be harmed, I never would have let that lizard become a man."

"It's not your fault," April said, obviously taken in by Samedi's Prince Charming routine.

I let the chance to tell Samedi it actually was his fault go by. "About what I need to know…"

"It'll cost you," Samedi said, looking at April. "That one," he nodded to the body on the floor, "barely entertained me for an hour."

"She's not for sale."

April went rigid and started walking toward Samedi, under his control.

"And who are you to keep me from taking her?" There was still humor in Samedi's voice, but a darker tone had been added to it, as if he was challenging me to try something.

"You know, I was going to try and do this the nice way," I pulled out the slightly warm ankh, "but if you insist on being a dick, I guess I'll just have to be the guy with the big silver ankh."

Samedi tried to get up, but I touched the ankh to his leg. There was a dull flash and he sat back down. April stopped moving.

"You do not know what you do." Samedi's voice had become deeper and seemed to be inside of my skull as well as outside. The god's features, thin to begin with, were now gaunt, as if his skin was just there to hide his bones and his eyes had disappeared into his skull.

"I know exactly what I do," I said harshly back to him. "And, while I appreciate you not telling the lizards about the whole reincarnation thing, I'd appreciate it more if you'd just tell me what I need to know so I can save the world and go to sleep. I even brought you some more of that rum to show I'm not a complete bastard."

Not moving my eyes or the ankh a millimeter from Samedi, I fished the bottle of rum out of my coat. I handed it to the god, who grabbed it.

Samedi uncorked the bottle and took a sip, savoring it as best he could. Some of the humanity returned to him, but his eyes remained empty hollows. "I won't kill you, Roger, but don't be tinking we're even."

"Fair enough," I said with a nod. "Now, I need to know where there's a gateway to naga-Hell around here, and how to get to it."

Samedi laughed. "So dat's what dat ol' snake is up to. Can't say I like it, but good for him."

"Put away the pom-poms, Baron. It's my guess that there are enough nagas in naga-Hell to make up for any followers he'd lose by killing off all of us humans, so he's okay with wiping us out. Which means you'd lose all of your worshippers, and you'd die pretty quick."

"Gods don't die quick, Detective. It takes us millennia. Eons sometimes if you're strong enough. But dis, it is a problem."

Samedi took another sip of his rum. "And, in answer to your other questions, de gateway, she's under the Evil House. Plain as day."

"Oh, better and better." I shook my head. "I always figured that it was a gateway to Hell; I just didn't know it was big lizard Hell."

I got up, keeping my ankh out but lowering it to my side. I looked at April, who was still stiff. "As much as I enjoy her like this, could you let her go in a minute so I can get this over with?"

"Let me have her, Roger. I could clothe her in dis one's flesh for de rest of the night." Samedi pointed to the body on the floor. "It would be a shame to lose one so pretty to dat place."

"She's already lost, Baron. Before you let her go, though, I do have another favor to ask you."

"You're getting bold, Roger."

"Fear of the world ending does that to a guy. I need you to follow these directions for me," I took out a pen and piece of paper, then scribbled some instructions on it. I handed the note to Samedi. "To the letter. Don't screw this up."

The Baron took it from me. "I'm not a messenger boy. Why should I do dis for you?"

"Just read the damn thing and you'll understand."

He looked it over. "You serious 'bout this?"

"You bet your drunk ass I am."

Samedi laughed. "Your balls musta grown 'bout two pounds tonight to do dis."

"You do what you've gotta," I said. "Will you do it for me?"

He thought it over. "Yes, if just for the entertainment I'm sure it will make."

"Thanks. You've got some pretty big ones yourself to agree to that. Now, if you could let her go?"

April relaxed and looked around. "What just happened?"

"The Baron was kind enough to answer some questions for me. And now we're leaving."

I nodded to Samedi. "Thanks, Baron. If I live through this, I'll try and set you up with the person I get that rum from."

Baron Samedi remained seated. "Good luck den, Roger, if just so I can get more of dis." He waved the bottle a little.

I smiled. "Damned alcoholic gods."

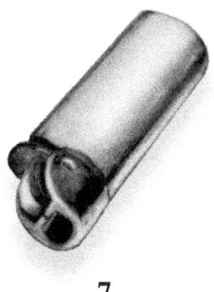

**7.**

We left Ron's house and headed out to the Sunbird. I grabbed my gun and a spare clip out of the glove compartment.

"A gun for ghosts?" April asked.

"You never know," I said, slamming the passenger side door. I slipped the gun and clip into my trench coat.

I decided to walk the hundred or so yards down Davis Street to the Evil House. Halfway there, April zoned out.

"Well, you made it further than I thought you would," I said to her.

We got to the Evil House without a problem. If anything, the place was worse than I remembered it up close. Two of the three steps leading up to its porch had broken in the middle, leaving jagged shards of wood, each one covered in something dark and brown, scattered about. The peeling paint, once blue, now looked like leprous skin rotting away from a diseased body. Its boarded-up picture window should have offered some sort of respite from the nightmarish thing, but some enterprising graffiti artist, sensing what really lurked here, had painted dozens of crimson eyes all over it. The paint had run, and each eye looked like it was crying blood. Something poked its black head out of a hole in the roof's peak, just above the shattered, second story window, screeched at me, then ducked back in. Ironically, the only thing in anywhere near good condition was the door.

April kept going, walking right through the front door. The surviving step gave me the definite impression that it was daring me to make the same mistake that two other people had made with the other steps. I took that dare and stepped as far to the right as I could, hoping that the little support provided by its rusty nails would last long enough to let me pass.

Once there, the blackened wood that made up the front porch didn't look any sturdier than the steps. Seeing no other choice, I walked across it, thinking light thoughts.

I tried the door. It was locked.

"Naturally," I muttered.

I took out my gun. "No time for subtlety."

The first bullet hit the door-frame, sending chunks of dry-rotted wood everywhere. The second hit the door itself, putting a good sized hole in it. And, finally, the third one hit the knob, knocking it out of the door. I kicked the door open and walked in.

Dark, yellow light that felt like it was shining directly on my soul, lighting up every nasty thing I'd ever done, seeped up through cracks in the floorboards, filling the hallway and illuminating a set of narrow stairs on my right that led up to the second floor and darkness. What was probably a living room at some point lay ahead of me, amply lit by the glow, letting me know which direction to go.

"At least he's a helpful destroyer of worlds," I said as I walked into the living room. The only things occupying it were a few scraps of newspaper and an odd, brown stain in the shape of Minnesota.

More light outlined a cheap wooden door to my right. A Master lock hung from it.

"Dammit, doesn't anybody trust people anymore?" I asked whoever, or whatever, ever might be listening in on me.

It only took me two shots to hit the lock.

I waited for my ears to stop ringing. I once got jumped by a clan of pissed off gnomes because I didn't wait for my eyes to adjust to the darkness of a cave; that taught me to wait out anything like that that put me at a disadvantage. While I waited, I put the gun away and pulled out my ankh. It just seemed like a better option in what would probably be close-quarters.

When the ringing finally went down enough, I opened the door and went down a set of rough-carved wooden stairs that looked like they'd been shoved into the dirt the basement had been dug out of. The occasional deep claw mark on the walls indicated that shovels hadn't been used to construct this basement originally, and probably neither had people. This created the very unpleasant possibility that the Evil House had been intentionally built over this spot with the express purpose of digging out whatever I was walking into and hiding it in plain sight until needed. And, given that the Evil House was over a hundred years old, that implied a hell of a lot of forethought on someone's part.

At the bottom, the stairs turned back at a small landing, then stopped at a partially excavated arch made of what looked like amber. It was wide enough for two people, or one naga, to walk through. At least some of the light filling the basement seemed to be coming from there, funneled up through it from somewhere underground.

As is to be expected from an older house, the basement itself was tiny, mainly taken up by a rusting, gutted-out boiler squatting in the middle of it like a metal toad. Most of the ocher light illuminating everything originated from somewhere inside of it, as if its pilot light had burrowed into the ground in an attempt to escape the Evil House.

I glanced around, hoping something less obviously a trap would show itself. The only other thing the basement contained, though, was a formerly secret room set into the far wall, its door blasted outward by gods only knew what kind of force, scattering singed papers and crumbled brick everywhere. A writing desk, still intact, sat in the room. I could sense a small presence in it, but not enough of one to be worried about.

"Let's get this over with," I said and walked up to the ruined boiler.

On one level, the one that most people would have seen, dust and rat droppings covered a flat slab of concrete inside it. On another level, the one that my "gift" let me see, sigils I didn't recognize, pulsing a dark, yellow light, surrounded a set of stone, spiral stairs descending into the ground. The steps, deeply worn in the middle by possibly millions of pairs of scaly feet, were taller than normal, made for nagas rather than humans. Despite the color of the light, a cold breeze smelling vaguely of damp earth blew out of the hole.

"Of course big lizard Hell is cold."

I awkwardly descended the steps, taking strides almost twice their normal length to do so, causing me to nearly stumble and fall a few times. It didn't help that I had to play keep-away with the ankh in my left hand. I had no idea what would have happened if it touched the wall or floor of a passage to a realm of evil dead and really didn't feel the need to experiment. This balancing/tumbling act must have gone on for at least a hundred yards into the ground before the steps finally stopped at another amber arch, apparently the source of all of the nasty light currently frying my soul. Deep, slash-like carvings in what I could only assume were nagaese, nagalish, nagaic, or whatever nagas called their language, covered it.

"If that says 'Abandon All Hope, etc.,' I'm inclined to agree."

"Actually," a voice said from behind me, causing me to jump, "it says, 'You who have lost all gleam to your souls, all sharpness to your hearts, come forward and be judged.' Or something along those lines. It doesn't really translate directly into English."

I turned, knowing who I'd see, but still surprised. Asklepiós, cleaned, groomed, and, thankfully dressed, sauntered down the final two steps like they'd been made specifically for him. Ropey, marathoner muscles slid under a pair of crimson snakeskin pants and a matching long-sleeved shirt as he walked up to me. I think they were clothes, anyway. Both clung tightly enough to him that they might have actually been his skin. You never knew with gods. My obsidian dagger, wrapped in what looked like pieces of his old rags, dangled from a leather strap at his side.

"I don't think I've ever seen you in clean clothes," I said neutrally, not really sure how to take his presence. On the one hand, I'd never known Asklepiós to be violent. On the other hand, he was one of Damballa's lackeys. And, on Shiva's third hand, a gentle warmth had begun flowing from the ankh, and a bluish, foxfire glow had flared up around it, something it only did in reaction to high levels of evil. This was possibly because of Asklepiós, but it was just as possibly because of naga Hell sitting on the other side of the arch.

"The end of the world seemed like a special enough occasion to bring them out."

"And you're here to make sure I don't get lost on the way to it?" I asked.

"Something like that."

I thought about arguing with him, possibly even threatening him so I didn't have to worry about getting stabbed in the back with my own knife, but decided against it. Asklepiós had harrowed a few underworlds in his time, if the myths were believable. He could wind up being useful. Hell, if Damballa had given him orders to make sure I made it to his little event, Asklepiós might even make a good meat shield between me and whatever was lurking down there.

"Fine. Just don't get in my way."

"Perish the thought, Detective."

A tingle passed over my skin as we walked under the arch, causing the hair on my arms to stand on end and my balls to retract almost into my stomach. Kind of like when the air conditioning kicks on, only more of a spiritual change of atmosphere.

"Welcome to the realm of damned nagas," I said. "Please check your baggage at the big stone arch."

I looked Asklepiós over. "You sure you're going to be okay in here wearing that?"

"The nagas wear the skins of their enemies as trophies, so yes, I will be just dandy. I'm surprised you didn't know that."

"I've never really been interested in whatever passes for culture for nagas," I said. "Keeping them from killing me and every other human on the planet's always been more important."

He had sense enough not to reply.

Life-sized nagas carved in various states of pain lined the rough-hewn, obsidian corridor past the arch, amber light glowing from their eyes the only source of illumination. What looked like barbed wire made of amber coiled into the flesh of one carving, the amber jaws of something big clamped on the midsection of another, and amber railroad-spike sized nails pierced the hands, feet and chest of another, posting it a foot from the ground. They continued on like this for some distance, curving with the passage and becoming more and more torturous, eventually culminating in various forms of dismemberment. The instrument of pain on each one was made of amber.

"I take it amber's their symbol for death?" I asked Asklepiós, turning away from a particularly gruesome statue being flayed alive by the amber talons of hands reaching out of the wall.

"And preservation. It has much the same function as salt in your culture. Though I can't comment on whether they ate it in the same heart-stopping quantities."

"So you're saying I should've been using amber against them all this time? Why am I just finding this out now?"

"Because you would rather make a sarcastic comment than actually pay attention to what someone says?" he suggested.

I was about to make a sarcastic comment to the contrary when the corridor opened up into a circular room big enough to make most stadiums sulk in a corner from inadequacy issues. A topaz half-moon that looked close enough to fall on us and pinpricks of winking light forming constellations the world hadn't seen in eons adorned its dark, curved ceiling. Twelve evenly spaced doorways stood open, waiting for us to choose one. And, lurking quietly in the center of the room, a pool of placid water tried its best to appear harmless.

*Dammit*, I thought, knowing full well what this was. All underworlds have various trials or security measures to keep out the living or unworthy spirits. They usually come in threes, but that's a number humans like. I had no idea what number nagas felt appropriate. I hoped it was one, but really doubted it.

"What do you think?" I asked Asklepiós. "Guardian spirit and sorter?"

He nodded. "What else? Unless there is a river hiding somewhere around here with a ferryman, guardians usually come first."

"Which door?"

Asklepiós nodded to the one directly across the room from us. "That doorway leads to the hell of Sraatsa."

"All right, follow me. Quietly. With luck we can sneak past him."

I inched around the edge of the room, watching each step and trying not to make any noise on the smooth floor. Asklepiós just sauntered along behind me a full foot away from the wall like he was out for a midnight stroll.

"What are you doing?" I whispered.

"It is impossible to avoid guardians, Detective. Trick, bribe, or overpower, yes, but never avoid. You always have to face them."

A stone slab slammed down in each doorway, shaking everything in the room but the water in the well and just about knocking me down.

"See?" he said, not a hair out of place.

The pool's surface roiled, sending a cold mist billowing over the floor, covering it in moments and giving gods only knew what the perfect hiding place if it wanted to sneak up on my hidden legs and eat them out from under me. Before I could worry too much about that, though, a bigger problem erupted from the sublimating water in the form of an albino naga head the size of a luxury car. Because gods always believe bigger is better, a body like Tokyo's worst nightmare, covered in enough scaly, leather armor to send an entire species into extinction,[8] rose and rose into the ancient night sky until it could almost reach the moon. It looked down at me with red eyes, flexing and unflexing sword-length claws, possibly with contempt or possibly to unsheathe its phone pole-length bone sword and hack me in two. It's hard to read facial expressions on normal-sized nagas. They're too different from humans. Deluxe-sized ones weren't any easier. Normally, I wouldn't have been too worried about a ghost, even one as intimidating as this one, but I'd stepped into a land of the dead, which meant that ghosts were very solid, and

---

[8] Like several gods' armors, its had more of an idealized look to it, though, like something that had been imagined into existence. Not that I wanted one, but I'd be willing to bet that a closer look would reveal the armor had no seams, having never actually been sewn together.

in this case, very dangerous.

"Sras to ahsra so," it said to me in a tone that told me I was right in assuming contempt.

"Let me guess. You're the guardian of naga Hell, and you either want a blood sacrifice, or fifty cents for the toll," I said.

It repeated its earlier statement, louder this time.

"Look, shouting's not gonna help me understand," I told it calmly.

"He is asking –" Asklepiós began.

"For an appropriate toll," I finished. "I know the drill."

The thought of just smacking the guardian with my ankh crossed my mind. He'd go down like a sugar cube hit with a fire hose if I got in a few shots, no doubt about that, but I wasn't real confident in my ability to dodge those claws. And the doors would probably stay closed. So I began to rifle through my pockets, looking for something useful. After rediscovering ten bucks I thought I'd lost, the bezoar, and the saint's pinky, I found a spare lighter. An idea popped into my head.

Guardian spirits fall into two categories: strong and dumb, like Cerberus, or smart and fast like most sphinxes. Both kinds will more than likely eat you if you give them half a reason, but they also come with the inclination to let you go if you're sufficiently clever. Naturally, the strong, dumb ones were easier to be clever at. Tall and gruesome looked to be in that category.

"You know," I told the guardian, "it's mighty cold in here."

I held myself and shivered to demonstrate the meaning.

Asklepiós groaned. "You are not seriously going to –"

I shushed him.

The guardian said nothing.

I flicked on my lighter.

That got its attention. It strode toward me and squatted down to get a better look.

I took my thumb off of the gas, causing the flame to go out.

It growled at me, exposing its teeth and giving me the opportunity to notice a second row that I hadn't seen earlier.

"All right, here's the deal," I said. "First, shrink down to non-Godzilla size."

I pointed at it, then held my hand flat and lowered it to the ground.

Without any kind of in-between, the guardian went from huge to only towering over me by a couple of feet, making my eyes water a bit from the rapid shift. It held out a hand and growled.

"Not yet, scaly. I'll give you this," I pointed at the lighter and then the guardian, "when you let me through the door." I pointed at myself and then the door.

As soon as I pointed to the door, the guardian grabbed the lighter from my hand, somehow managing to not take off my arm. The door we wanted slid open.

"Thanks," I said, leaving the guardian flicking the lighter on and off.

"I cannot believe that worked," Asklepiós said as we headed toward the exit. "I swear that trick is older than me."

"Yeah, it's almost like I know what I'm doing. I think I liked you better as a drunk, Asklepiós. This arrogance is getting old."

"Not arrogance, Detective. Tedium. When you have gone through this story as many times as I have, it gets tiresome. There are so few surprises anymore."

This corridor didn't have any decorations, just naked obsidian scored with thousands of claw marks, like countless nagas had been dragged through it unwillingly. It went fairly straight for a few hundred yards, an ever-present amber glow emanating from somewhere I couldn't identify. And I'd been around long enough to know better than to ask too many questions about little things like that. The answers tended to involve things like sacrificed children, or, on one occasion, the siphoned-off belief energy of Apollo. That debacle was why the Hidden Gardens of the Gyre were now the prison wasteland called the Gardener's Void.

Eventually, after going from straight to a half-dozen twists and turns that felt like they should have overlapped each other several times, the corridor opened up into a massive cavern that had me wondering for a moment if I'd wandered onto a set for *Journey to the Center of the Earth*. Bushes and ferns I'd never seen before covered the floor, and trees sprouted up and over the low growers, their tops disappearing into the mists obscuring the ceiling. With so much lush greenery, the scene looked almost tropical, but, if anything, this cavern was colder than the first one. And the only thing I smelled was stale, wet air, confirming that everything there was only a ghost. Ghosts, and ghostly illusions, never have an odor to them, no matter how real they seem. If you can smell it, it's something else.

The ghost plants and the cold didn't overly concern me, but the shrieks and growls coming from large, most likely hungry, animals hiding in the cavern did. And, with us being out of the city, I couldn't pick them out very well with my "gift."

"Ah, dammit," I said and backed into the corridor enough so that nothing huge could fit in it.

"Now this," Asklepiós said, smiling, "this is different. Someone with some imagination put this trial together."

"You're kidding, right? It's just Cerberus with scales and vegetation."

Which made the terrifying image of a three-headed tyrannosaurus rex guarding the next tunnel entrance pop into my head.

"You are thinking of a three-headed dinosaur, aren't you?" Asklepiós asked.

"Maybe."

"If it is as dim as Cerberus, then I wouldn't worry too much. Three heads may give him an intimidating appearance, but they really get in the way of each other more than anything else."

"If you think you can march us through this, be my guest."

He shrugged. "If I could I would. It would be much faster. But this is your adventure, Detective. I'm just along for the ride."

I wasn't sure how to take that. It implied that Asklepiós had come along under his own free will instead of at Damballa's urging. Why he wouldn't just come out and tell me that, I had no idea. Aside from standard god obstinacy, holding his cards so close to his vest made no sense. Well, less sense than most godly motives.

I decided to let him have his secrets. For the moment, at any rate.

I took out the remains of my cigar and lit it with my spare lighter. You only have to nearly get killed by a horde of ghostly bikers once from lack of lighter fluid to start carrying a spare one. Once I had an acrid cloud of nastiness around myself big enough to make Asklepiós take a few steps back, I put the lighter away, took a firm grip on my ankh, and started forward, wilting ghostly plants with every step.

The loud, crashing sound of something big shoving its way through the foliage came from my left, accompanied by an even louder roar and quick, even tremors large enough to set my teeth rattling. I took this as my cue to run, knowing full well there was a good chance I'd be dead before the dinosaur hunting me, because that's what it had to be in naga Hell, even needed to lean down to my level and be affected by the smoke. Asklepiós, apparently worried enough by the potential of becoming dino-chow to lose some of his nonchalance, kept up with me.

About a hundred yards ahead of us was the corridor out. Naturally, another stone slab blocked off its entrance.

"Damn," I said as I stopped.

Without even breaking stride, Asklepiós turned and ran back to the corridor we'd come out of. I followed at top speed, risking a glance behind me. A head about the size of a small car appeared through the foliage. Its scales, most likely olive green when the thing had been alive, looked closer to the color of pickle juice now. It stopped, sniffed the air, and looked my way, staring at me for a moment with one of its beady little eyes like I was the last bit of meat on the planet, something I'd be willing to bet it knew a little about. It roared, showing off machete-length teeth, probably just for effect, and came at me.

Leave it to the nagas to actually have a ghostly tyrannosaurus rex as a guardian. Least it only had one head.

Puffing, wheezing, and swearing, I made it to the corridor just as the tyrannosaur reached me. It snapped and growled, trying to push its head into the narrow hallway as I stood there getting my breath back.

"How can you be the Detective and be this out of shape?" Asklepiós asked, leaning casually against the wall.

"Not...all of us...can be gods," I managed.

"You're barely human, Roger. Humans can run a few meters without nearly passing out."

I drew a full blast of smoke into my mouth then blew it out at him. It would've been more impressive if the smoke hadn't flowed onto the floor like water, but he got the point and backed away.

After a couple minutes, I said, "Shut up," and walked up to the dinosaur, just out of its reach, and smacked it on the nose with the ankh.

"Bad lizard. Go away."

It jumped back with a scream loud enough to set me vibrating, then just stood there, not quite sure what to do.

"That's certainly a novel way of dealing with a guardian," Asklepiós said.

"Nobody's ever done that, have they?" I shouted out from the safety of the corridor. "Well, they should have. Bad lizard! No dinner!"

Hearing the tone of my voice, possibly sensing what it meant, the tyrannosaur roared again and tried to get at me one more time. And I smacked it on the nose one more time.

"Stupid lizard. Go away so I can save the world."

It jumped back with another scream and left.

"It's a good thing Samedi didn't come with us," I said as we moved on, following the path I'd made earlier. "He'd want to make a pet out of that thing."

"We would never hear the end of that. A century and a half later, and he still asks people to come back to his place to see his twenty-foot wyrm."

I rolled my eyes. "I swear, if I hear him use that line one more time I'm going to call Thor over to kill that thing."

We reached the spot where we'd had to turn and run. Sickly yellow light oozed out of the tunnel's opening like honey. Apparently giving the dinosaur a few love taps with my ankh and making it run away satisfied whatever conditions this trial had been set up for. Probably a test of physical prowess or something.

Or it was just a trick. Twenty yards away from the opening, the tyrannosaur crashed out of the trees at a full sprint. I didn't even waste time swearing. I just ran as fast as my out-of-shape legs would carry me, making the door just as the tyrannosaur chomped at me and missed me by inches. Asklepiós, of course, was already there.

I turned, weighed the benefits of actually trying to destroy the thing, and decided that I didn't have the time. The return trip, assuming there would be one, was a different story.

"I'll come back for you."

This corridor was made entirely out of amber, backlit by gods knew what. Trapped in the walls, the ceiling, and the floor, were the bodies of countless nagas of various colorations, going further and further back, one upon another, until I couldn't make anything out. I walked up to one for a closer inspection and its eyes darted to me, focusing on me with all the built-up rage that eons of imprisonment generates. Understandably, I jumped back.

"Looks like we're in their version of the ninth circle of Hell," I said. "How's it feel to be my Virgil?"

"You are not Dante," Asklepiós said flatly. "And we are not on our way to Heaven after a brief viewing of Damballa."

"Did that whole thing really happen?" I asked. I'd never come across a reference to the validity of *The Divine Comedy* in any of the previous Detectives' files. Not that I'd been looking all that hard. The truth behind pieces of Western literature really only mattered when something awful related to one of them was about to happen. The Water Babies incident springs to mind. I still hate Victorian literature for that one.

"Yes, most definitely. There are at least three gates to Hell in Italy, one very close to where Dante was living at the time. Though not quite as many of Dante's political rivals were down there as he would have liked us to believe. Especially the still-living ones."

I had to laugh at that. Made me almost start to like Asklepiós again. Not enough to forgive him for helping cause this mess, though. Not by a long shot.

We trudged on through the corridor, countless eyes burning into us, for what seemed like forever. Finally, we reached a cavern so deep and wide that I couldn't see the other side.

We stopped walking. I don't know about Asklepiós, but I had to take it in. I've seen some truly impressive and terrifying places over the years. The vast forest-cities of Faerie, the death-eating necropolis carved out of Detroit's salt mines, and the toilets of the Forgotten Bar all come to mind. I'm not sure where this place sat on that list, but it definitely hit the top ten. The ochre light, feverish before, took on a cold, delirious intensity, making my skin feel hot and thick on my flesh, like a too-tight winter jacket intentionally trying to suffocate me. The immobilized bodies of thousands of trapped nagas flowed through the cavern's amber walls, holding the monsters prisoner while dark shapes swam in the depths of rock, free to do whatever they pleased. And it seemed what they wanted most was to devour the souls a piece at a time. As I watched, something resembling a dolphin, but with long, sinewy arms ending in serrated talons instead of flippers, slashed off chunks of spirit-flesh from random nagas and shoved the bloody meat into a mouth filled with hundreds of barbed, needle-like teeth. Other, larger shapes hunted further back in the amber, thankfully too far away to make out clearly.

"These are the worst of the damned," Asklepiós said. "Pacifists and scavengers too weak-hearted in life to kill, making them a burden to their clans."

I stopped. "Wait. You're telling me that they're in naga-hell because they *wouldn't* kill anyone?"

"Yes. Nagas are carnivores and warriors, and any who got the silly notion that killing another being was wrong would not be able to defend their clan and had to rely on others to provide them with food or steal it. And naga society never really developed much past the hunting and fishing level, so theft of food was the worst crime to them, followed by cowardice. So here they've been for eons, starving and slowly being devoured over and over again by ichthyodemons and their kin. And perhaps others. Rumor has it that, sensing the end of the nagas, Rohrons, the lord of Sraatsa, sank himself and his court into the deepest trenches of his amber sea."

"And these are the guys Damballa wants to let loose? They must be ten kinds of crazy by now."

Asklepiós nodded. "And very, very hungry."

Then an awful thought popped into my head. "Wait a minute. I know the gateway opens up once in a while and sucks in the occasional human spirit. Did any of them make it down here?"

"I would imagine so. Not many humans in this area kill their own food, so they would most likely get sorted into this hell."

"Shit. That means that we have to save them."

Asklepiós smiled in that way parents do when their kids ask if their dead pet is ever going to wake up. "Detective, there are thousands of spirits locked away in these walls. Do you really think that you can rescue the few dozen humans mixed among them? The only one who could possibly do that is Rohrons. And he's probably in no better shape than his inmates."

I knew he was right. Still didn't make me feel better about the situation, but awful truths are part of being Kalamazoo's Detective.

Speaking of awful truths, Asklepiós's little speech brought up something. "How do you know all of that? There's no way Damballa would've told you."

He sighed. "I'm old, Detective. Not naga old, but most definitely older than you monkeys. You honestly didn't think that, in sixty-six million years, something else never stood up and thought about itself, did you? Just be happy that they were mammals, too."

"So you are here to help me."

"You? No. You're a horrible little creature that I would just as soon see gone. But, as you were so kind to point out earlier this evening, I am not a killer. I've seen one race wander off into extinction. I would rather not help push another one into it."

I didn't quite buy his story. Gods are incapable of telling the whole truth, as far as I can tell. But enough of it sounded at least plausible that I didn't feel like calling him on it.

"Fine. Just don't do anything that gets me killed until after we've saved the world."

A path went off to the left, slanting downward along the edge of the cavern and the vast, nearly empty plain below. Some sort of yellow structure surrounding a tower sat toward the middle, but I couldn't quite make it out at that distance. Not that I could even tell how far away it was, truthfully. The complete lack of anything to use for reference made it impossible.

"The great fortress Sraatsa-kha," Asklepiós said, seeing me squint. "Built by Rohrons from the carcass of his mother, the sea-dragon Hitara, who he slew with the shard of his broken sword, Dolok, the God-Slayer."

"I'm guessing that's the big tower in the middle of the castle."

Asklepiós nodded. "Now the Damnation Lock."

"Probably keeps the dead on their side of the wall."

He nodded again.

"His mother?"

"Read the story for yourself, Detective. It is all there if you would simply open your eyes."

I looked. I didn't see a story, but I could just make out April, plodding her way down the path toward the fortress.

"The only thing I see is a dead stripper I'd like to have a word with."

A loud growl came from somewhere below, followed by a flash of yellow light shooting from the tower into the ceiling, then silence.

"Damballa is starting his attack on the Damnation Lock," Asklepiós said, a little worry creeping into his voice. "We need to hurry."

By the time we caught up to April, I could make out most of what we were walking toward. I'd seen a few buildings with bone furnishings over the years [9], but never an entire fortress. The scale impressed me, if nothing else. Time-browned ribs three-stories tall made up a circular wall that could have encompassed a football stadium. Opaque amber, thankfully devoid of large, pissed off lizards, filled the gaps. The narrow skull of something, its wide-open jaw lined with teeth the size of your average sports car, served as the entrance. Still-living eyes with green, slit irises watched April approach.

"She's the third test, isn't she?" I asked, stopping.

"Yes, there are always three tests," Asklepiós replied. Then he smiled. "Except when the goddess harrowing the underworld is Ishtar. Then it's however many it takes to get her naked."

Having met Ishtar, a goddess that could make a ninety-year-old monk renounce his vow of chastity, I had to smile, too.

"You're making that up."

---

[9] The real entrance to Asylum Tower, for example, the one that leads to the hidden operating theatre where so many people died an inch at a time under the 'care' of the thing that called itself the Mind Arbiter, is made of the interlocking skeletons of former inmates.

He put a finger to his lips. "Shh. Watch."

April stopped for a moment, held up two fingers, then trudged through the gate unmolested.

"The giant dead snake-thing is going to ask me a question in my head, isn't she?" I asked.

"How else would it communicate with you? It lacks a tongue."

I wanted to argue this with him, pointing out how much I hated having things talk to me in my head, especially dead things, but I couldn't fault his logic.

"Might as well get this over with," I said and headed toward the gate.

The eyes focused in on me. A surprisingly pleasant female voice in my head said, "Humans aren't allowed here. Leave."

"I happen to know that there are at least two humans in there, so let me in," I said, only a little surprised the inert, ancient god spoke English. She was in my head, after all. Gods only knew what else she'd learned poking around in there.

"There are three. But two were under the protection of Progenitor Danaido, and one knew the ritual."

"Progenitor?"

"Sire of one of the ten naga tribes, lord of their newly dead."

"And royal pain in my ass."

I ran my hand through my hair in frustration. "Look, I need in there, and I know that there's a way for you to let me pass. Let's just get on with it so I can save the world and go home."

"No," Hitara said. "Leave this place. Now."

I looked at Asklepiós, who just shrugged.

"Maybe you need to say please," he said.

I was willing to try anything at that point. "Fine. Please let me in."

"No, Detective. Leave, and do not bother me again."

Asklepiós, seeing me wind up to throw my ankh at the skull, quickly said, "Ask her one more time."

Understanding fought its way through my sleep-deprived brain. "That's three times you've denied me entry. Now ask me whatever question you've gotta ask and let me in."

"How many have you killed?"

"What?"

"How many have you killed?" Hitara asked again, her voice hard. "It's a simple question, Detective. Answer it to pass. Or don't, and I eat you."

I've done a lot of horrible things to protect Kalamazoo, many only known to me and my victim. The only things that kept them from driving me nuts was not thinking about them and focusing instead on the next horrible thing I had to do.

"No, I get it," I said, trying to bluff my way through how much the question rattled me. "You're the door to the naga hell for pacifists, so the question lets the person, naga, whatever, trying to get in show off their record and make sure they're not here to let out one of the damned. I'm just confused about the time period. I mean, just today, or total?"

"Over the course of your life."

"I'm not going to sit here and list off all of my sins for you, Hitara. You're in my head, so look for yourself."

And she did. Not gently, either. The force of her ancient, completely inhuman mind shoving its way into the corners of mine dropped me to one knee. I'd like to say that the tears running down my face came from my brain almost being pushed out of my skull, but I'd be lying. I got to see the final moments of half a dozen gods, scores of supernatural critters of all shapes and sizes, a few humans, and I don't even know how many ghosts. Only a small percentage of those deaths were of people or things I cared about. Lucky me.

After what felt like forever, Hitara backed off and lowered her jaw.

"You may pass, Hunter," she said. "Honor the cowardly dead with your presence and keep them from escaping their rightful torment."

I managed to stand with a minimal amount of wobbliness. "That's the plan. Come on, Asklepiós. Let's go stop another Armageddon. Hopefully you'll be more helpful than you have been so far."

"I prevented you from taking a rather rash action," he said as we passed through Hitara's mouth and into a dark corridor with an amber light at the end. "I would call that helping."

"You couldn't just tell me to ask her three times?"

"Do I ask you how to heal? Then do not ask me how to do your job. Learn the traditions and stories, Detective."

"I do know the traditions, Asklepiós. But, in case you haven't noticed, I'm running on empty. Something you should know about. So excuse me if I don't remember every gods damned myth about breaking into the underworld."

I was just about to start up on round two of my tirade when we passed out of the corridor. Self-preservation told me to shut the hell up. Not a hundred yards away from us, the Damnation Lock jutted from the ground, a spike of amber tall enough it'd need warning lights for planes. About a hundred armored nagas surrounded it, their full attention focused on the ivory snake wrapped around the spire in coils probably fifteen feet thick.

"Damballa," I said under my breath. "Guess I should have brought a bigger urinal cake."

I looked for the kid and Beth, but couldn't see them. April was in full view, though, still doing her job of leading me onward.

"SOON, MY FAITHFUL, YOUR BROTHERS AND SISTERS SHALL BE FREED!" Damballa said in a voice that shook the cavern.

The nagas started hissing and roaring.

Damballa looked down at me with a head the size of a freight engine. "AS SOON AS THE SPIRITUALIST ARRIVES."

Two-hundred-plus slitted eyes turned to me, letting me know just how a sheep on its way to the slaughter feels.

"Detective, Old Snake," I shouted up to him, wanting to regain some control of the situation, even if only in my head. "And I'll be over there in my own sweet time. Don't get your scales in a bunch."

April stopped and turned to look at me. "Don't talk to him like that! He's going to fix the world."

"About time you quit acting like you were doped up," I said. "You know, if you wanted me down here so bad you should've just asked instead of messing around with me like this."

April, who was about to say something else, broke off as if I'd just stolen her thunder.

"Yes, I knew you were working for them. There's more than one kind of snake. At first I hoped it was just coincidence that the kid was your boyfriend. My fault for forgetting there's no such thing as coincidences, I guess. I was pretty sure that you were working together, though, when the nagas and that kid were able to find me so quickly. But I didn't figure it out completely until you stuck around after we found out how you'd died. You appeared in my closet asking me to find out who killed you, so you should've moved on when we did. But you stayed. That's when I realized that they must've been using you to trace me somehow. The how clicked when I grabbed your purse and looked at your license. They used your true name to keep track of your movements and mine."

I looked at Asklepiós. "There, see? I do know how to do my job."

"Did I say anything?" he asked.

April put her hands on her hips. "Who –"

I held up a finger. "Hush. Big people talking.

"What did you promise her?" I shouted to Damballa. "A new body? Eternal youth?"

"BOTH. AND WHEN MY FOLLOWERS ARE FREE, SHE SHALL HAVE THEM."

"And then you'll kill her again," I said so that only April could hear.

"He won't do that," she protested. "He's a good god."

"Bullshit," I said. "I know gods, and that's exactly how they think."

I shooed April forward as she just stared at me, trying to figure out a comeback.

"I take exception to that," Asklepiós said. At least he had the decency to only pretend to sound shocked. "I am here helping you save the world, after all."

"Only because I guilted you into it."

"Still, here I am."

Damballa moved his head a little closer to us. "GLYKON? WHY DID YOU FOLLOW HIM, LITTLE SNAKE? YOUR PART IN THIS IS FINISHED."

Which added some credulity to Asklepiós's story, though it still didn't necessarily make it true.

Asklepiós visibly tensed at the insult. "To make certain that you don't back out our deal, wyrm."

"I REPAY MY DEBTS, GODLING. I HAVE SPENT MILENNIA AWAITING THE CHANCE TO REPAY MY FINAL DEBT TO MY CHILDREN, AND IT IS HERE AT LAST. THE THREE BRIDGES BETWEEN DEATH – THE ONE WHO SPEAKS WITH THE DEAD, THE ONE WHO BRIDGES THE DEAD, AND THE ONE WHO RETURNED FROM THE DEAD – WILL ALLOW MY CHILDREN TO FINALLY RETURN TO THIS WORLD AND RECLAIM IT."

I ignored them both. Asklepiós was obviously just winding Damballa up. And any comments on my part toward Damballa would only lengthen his monologue on the greatness and inevitability of his plan. Not that he needed encouragement. Felt like he'd saved up all those words from the other times he'd talked to me in clipped sentences, with interest.

"BEFORE THE ASTEROID WAS BROUGHT, MY FOLLOWERS RULED THIS WORLD. IF NOT FOR THAT, THEY WOULD BE OUT AMONG THE STARS BY NOW, SPREADING MY

WORSHIP WHEREVER THEY WENT. WE HAVE BEEN DENIED OUR BIRTHRIGHT FOR FAR TOO LONG."

"He's awfully chatty when he's about to destroy the world," I said to Asklepiós.

Then what he'd just confessed sank in. "Wait a minute. Did he say 'brought'?"

"I believe so."

I couldn't help myself. I had to laugh at the stupidity of the whole situation. "You were trying to generate more belief for yourself by causing the end of the world. But there was no one there to stop it, was there?"

If he heard me, he didn't acknowledge it.

"AFTER THE GREAT DEATH, I SLEPT FOR EONS UNTIL SENTIENT LIFE THAT COULD WORSHIP AND BELIEVE IN ME FINALLY RETURNED, SUCH AS IT WAS. YOU HAIRLESS MONKEYS HAVE NOWHERE NEAR THE SPIRIT OF MY CHILDREN. EVEN THOSE SENT TO SRAATSA ARE BETTER THAN YOUR KIND."

"Your people never worshipped him?" I asked Asklepiós.

"They were not people, Detective. And they never reached the place of his slumber, so he never had a chance to infect them with his presence." I looked up at Damballa. "I'm sorry, were you saying something?"

"YOUR BARBS MEAN LITTLE TO ME, SPIRITUALIST. SOON, YOU WILL BE GONE. BUT, IF IT HELPS, THINK OF IT AS AVOIDING THE RUSH."

"Oh ha fucking ha," I said. "Like I haven't heard that one before..."

As we neared the crystal, I could see Beth and the kid bound to it at ground level. An empty set of leather restraints that looked like they were just about my size hung next to Beth.

"So, am I supposed to strap myself in, or what?" I asked April.

"No," she replied. "Our lord will place them upon you."

"How nice of him."

"About time you got here," Beth shouted to me.

"What, you thought I was just going to leave you here to have all of the fun by yourself?" I said back to her. "Besides, I couldn't stand you up on our date."

"Some date. Next time I get to pick where we go."

"So you're saying you'd go out with me again?" I asked with a touch of seriousness.

"If you save the world, I'd be more than happy to go out with you again."

I looked up at the giant snake that could probably eat a dragon in one bite, then at the gathered throng of nagas. "You don't impress easily, do you?"

"Gotta work if you want to go out with me."

I sighed. "I guess it's worth it."

"Not to interrupt this touching scene, but were you planning on actually doing something about this situation?" Asklepiós asked.

"Already am. But, yeah, I guess I should do my bit."

I looked up to Damballa, who was watching me with eyes the size of dinner tables. "Are we going to be sacrificed?" I asked him.

"YES. THEN YOUR SPIRITS WILL ENTER THE CRYSTAL AND BRIDGE THE REALMS OF THE DEAD AND THE LIVING."

"Great, that's what I thought." I pulled out my gun and shot at the kid, killing him with the second bullet.

"FOOLISH. HE WAS GOING TO DIE ANYWAY. AN EARLY DEATH MEANS LITTLE TO ME."

"Uh-huh," I said as I pulled a urinal cake out of my other pocket.

As soon as the kid's ghost stepped out of his skinsuit, I said his name, promptly sucking it into the urinal cake.

"No!" April screamed. She rushed at me, her right hand held high. Claws like some great cat's popped out, showing a mastery of her ghostly form that surprised me.

Asklepiós darted in for the interception, grabbing her around the waist and picking her up like she was made of paper.

"Don't just stand there, Detective," he said, arms straining to keep their grip on April's struggling spirit. "Her spirit is stronger than it appears."

"Strap her onto the Damnation Lock, then," I said. "She can have my place."

I ran up to Beth and started undoing the straps around her wrists.

"How was that?" I asked her.

"Not bad. Now, how are we supposed to get out of her without Damballa and his kin killing us and just breaking that kid's new home?"

"I'm working on it."

"A little help," Asklepiós said as he struggled to bind April to the lock. "She keeps wriggling out of my grip."

"A great big god like you can't lace that tiny thing up?" Beth asked.

Something in Asklepiós seemed to snap for a moment. He slammed April's spirit into the lock with one hand, dazing her for a second, and held her there. A golden nimbus of godly energy sprang up around him. April screamed.

"Am I the only one who realizes the seriousness of this situation? Instead of forcing me to waste my strength on petty tasks, one of you awful little creatures could tighten her bonds."

"Fine," I said, strapping April in. "There. Happy?"

His divine fire disappeared. "Immensely. What is our next move?"

I looked up, expecting something. After two seconds of not seeing it, I said, "How about we run really fast for a while?"

Neither of them bothered to answer as we made for the gate. The nagas, apparently not worried by the situation, just stood there.

"PATHETIC."

Damballa moved for us, slamming down a large coil in our path with more speed than anything that large had the right to move. The shockwave nearly knocked Beth and me to the ground, but we managed to keep our feet under us. Asklepiós, of course, didn't even look rattled.

"Anytime now, Samedi," I said as the coil moved in on us.

"Damballa, my brother," came Baron Samedi's voice from the darkness above us. "Dis game of yours, she's over."

Damballa stopped and looked up. "YES, 'BROTHER,' IT IS. AND I AM ABOUT TO WIN IT.

"STOP THEM, MY CHILDREN, AND HOLD THEIR SPIRITS WHILE I ATTEND TO THIS GODLING."

"You think I would come here all alone?" Samedi asked. He laughed. "The drink has not affected me that much, Brother."

A flood of ghosts hundreds strong rolled through Hitara's jaws, with Taylor and her group of women at the lead. From above, Baron Samedi dropped on top of Damballa's head and started riding it like a bucking bronco. Occasionally, there was the flash of something metallic that I couldn't make out.

"What did you do?" Beth asked.

"Got a certain alcoholic god to convince most of the ghosts in town to play cavalry for us. I'm dying to know how he got them past the gateway…"

"Not bad."

"Glad you approve. Now go. Get to the corridor and you should be safe."

"I don't think so. I'm done playing damsel in distress. I'm staying here with you to beat these things down."

I ducked as a naga took a swipe at me with its claws. Apparently the ban on killing me had been lifted. "I'm pretty short on effective weapons. All I've got left are my ankh and my gun. What are you going to use?"

Beth gave a nearby naga a solid punch just below its stomach. It screamed and fell down, clutching itself.

"Unlike you, I know where to hit these things and make it count," Beth said. "Well, Rosa does, anyway."

"Then here, you take the ankh and I'll take the gun." I tossed the ankh to her.

"Just make sure you point it away from me," Beth told me as she nailed another naga with the ankh, causing a small flash of light.

"Yeah, yeah, yeah."

Apparently tired of our inability to take the end of the world seriously, Asklepiós had dialed up his holy light again and waded into the nagas. For their part, they all ran screaming from him and at the human ghosts. They couldn't all escape, though. Occasionally, he'd catch one and it would burst into golden flames, burning from the inside until nothing was left.

"You owe me one for this, dick," Taylor shouted over to me.

I shot wildly at a naga, hitting the one behind it in the shoulder. It disintegrated into a fine, blue mist. "I wish people would stop telling me that," I shouted back. "I'm saving the damned world, after all. Have a heart."

"What kind of bullets do you have in there?" Beth asked after I shot another naga, this time in the leg, and it evaporated.

"I got them blessed by Ares last time he swung through town. He appreciated the irony enough to actually do it without making me force him."

The fighting continued. There were a lot of human ghosts, but none of them had the size, training, or sheer pent-up ferocity of the nagas. Dozens of humans would dogpile a single naga only to be thrown off like they weren't even there. I saw a particularly brutal naga wade into the crowd of human ghosts, swinging its clawed hands like sickles, decapitating and disemboweling men and women as casually as if he were swatting away flies. Occasionally, just for variety, he'd pick a man up, tear him in two, and use the halves to beat back a wave of attackers. It became obvious pretty fast that my side wasn't going to win this.

"This isn't working," I said to Beth as we fought side by side. "For every one of them we take down, they take down five of ours."

"Why aren't all of these ghosts being sucked into the crystal?" Beth asked me. "You know as well as I do that's where they've been going. If we can get it to do its job again, this fight will be over pretty damn fast."

I looked over to the crystal. Damballa, as much as he was bucking and rolling in an attempt to get Samedi off of himself, still had his tail wrapped around part of it.

"It's Damballa. Somehow he's blocking the effect by holding onto the crystal," I said. "We've got to get him off of it."

We took off toward the crystal but were brought up short when a group of five nagas, all armored and carrying serrated bone swords, stepped out of the melee to block us.

"Kortash, Detective," the red-scaled naga in the middle said.

I shot at him and actually managed to hit the center of his chest, knocking him flat on his back before he went up in smoke.

"I don't have time for this, boys," I said.

"Hor ta go shakor lah asangis go hruk, Detective," the brown scaled naga on the left end said.

"He says that he's pretty sure at least one of them will get through to you before you can kill all of them," Beth translated.

"You speak their language?"

"Rosa does, but she won't tell me how she knows it. She says a girl should have her secrets."

They charged us. I clipped one, causing its essence to disperse, and managed to get off a shot at another, but it went wild. When one got into clubbing range, Beth snaked in under its reach and swung, knocking it backward a good ten feet with a bright flash. The other two swung their swords at me. I stepped to my left, avoiding one sword slash. The other sliced down my chest, leaving a thin trail of blood and a torn shirt in its wake.

"Ahh," I shouted, then shot the one that had cut me.

"It's just a cut," Beth told me, hitting the naga that had missed me and sending it sprawling backward.

"I'm fine, thanks for asking," I replied.

"You'll be okay, quit whining. Now come on."

A few other nagas tried to get in our way without backup. They either got shot by me or clubbed by Beth. Once we reached the crystal, we were faced with another problem.

"How do we get him off?" Beth asked.

"I'm fresh out of grease, so I suggest we just beat on him until he gets the idea," I said.

"Leave him alone!" April shouted from behind us.

"Y'know," I started as I turned, "at this point I don't even care how you got loose. I'm just sick of dealing with you."

"And I'm sick of you always bitching," April said with a sneer. "I hate this, and I want to go to sleep, and this sucks. Why don't you just shut the hell up?"

"I've been saying that for years," Beth muttered.

"We are on the same side, right?" I asked Beth.

"Well, screw you," April continued as if neither of us had said anything. "Now I can just kill you and finally get you out of my life."

April ran at me, claws out again. I stepped aside just as she got to me, letting her run into Damballa. The force of the collision caused her to stumble backward and fall.

"Life?" I said down to her. "You still can't get it through your head that you're dead, can you? Hit her on the head with the ankh, Beth."

"A please would be nice," she said as she clocked April on her left cheek with a blow that would have snapped her neck if she hadn't already been dead, leaving a large, ankh-shaped burn.

"Please, and thank you," I told her. "Now, about Damballa…"

I turned back to the god and emptied my clip into the huge piece of his tail to no effect. After I was finished, Beth started beating on it with the ankh. With every flash, Damballa shuddered, until finally his grip loosened.

Behind us, silence erupted.

We turned around and saw every ghost frozen in place. Nagas about to bite, rend, or claw unfortunate humans in two, humans tearing nagas limb from limb with sheer numbers, all stood caught in their last acts. Asklepiós, his glow slightly dimmer, took the opportunity to rip the head off of the unresisting naga he'd been fighting. The other nagas dropped their victims or stepped away from their potential slayers and shuffled forward, entering the crystal when they reached it. The humans remained where they were.

"You had Samedi do something to the people, didn't you?" Beth asked, the ankh glowing a fierce blue and smoking in her hands.

"Hey, give me some credit. I'm tired and grumpy, but that doesn't mean I want all of the people who were nice enough to fight the big lizards with us to wind up in naga Hell with them. He told them to stop whatever they were doing and go home if something other than him tried to call to them. And since he's a human god, they're listening to him instead of the crystal."

I bent down and dragged April to the crystal. "I do want her in there, though." As soon as her head touched the lock, her body disappeared. Looking in, I could see her falling into its depths, her body limp and soon to be food for the monsters that scared monsters.

"She's not going to be happy when she wakes up," I said. "But hopefully it'll teach her not to make deals with gods."

Damballa clutched the Damnation Lock again, and Beth smacked him again.

"Remind me not to piss you off too seriously," she told me.

"NO! STOP, MY CHILDREN! DO NOT GO!"

Specifically designed to imprison them, the crystal's call to the nagas was stronger than the god's order. We stood aside to let the nagas shamble their way to the crystal and the human ghosts shamble their way out of the cavern. Every time Damballa tried to get a grip on it again, Beth hit him and Samedi beat him in the head.

"It's time we get out of here," I said once they were all in. "I'm not sure if Samedi can beat him after all of the naga belief Damballa's been sucking up down here."

"Good point," Beth agreed.

"Asklepiós!" I shouted. "We're leaving!"

"NO, SPIRITUALIST, YOU ARE NOT," Damballa said. "MY CHILDREN WILL NOT LET YOU."

I was just about to point out that all of his children were now snack food for demons when an awful thought occurred to me.

"Samedi! Get him away from the lock! He's going to open it!"

"I DO NOT HAVE TIME TO KILL ALL OF YOU, BUT I CAN STILL SET THEM FREE."

"He don't have reins up here, Detective," Samedi yelled down to us. "I can't keep him back."

"But he can't open the lock," Beth said. "He'd need...oh. Oh no."

"Yeah. As a god of the dead, he's the ultimate bridge between worlds. And he can sacrifice himself with the giant, god-slaying chunk of sword he's conveniently wrapped around."

With one, powerful heave of his coils, Damballa threw his neck onto the Damnation Lock's point, severing his head cleanly from his body. Blood rained down on us like a torrent, covering Asklepiós, Beth, and me in a sheen of gore. But nothing else. The amber ground absorbed every drop of the horrific deluge that hit it until the only evidence left of the atrocity was dribbling off of us. Even the blood on Asklepiós was disappearing as the god took that little bit of Damballa's power into himself.

Damballa's body slowly tumbled to the ground, like it now lacked most of its substance and was only the frailest remains of something long dead. Samedi rode the snake god's head as it wafted to the ground, whooping and hollering the whole way.

"Dat was some good times," he said, all smiles.

Tremors rocked the ground, causing spider-web cracks to appear across the amber around us.

"And, like all good times, we're 'bout to pay for dem," Samedi continued.

"Not if Asklepiós fixes this," I told him.

"I cannot fix this," Asklepiós said as he joined us. "The best we can do is seal this place off from the world of the living and hope for the best."

"Bullshit," I said. "You can resurrect Damballa before this gets too far along."

"That won't work," Beth said. "His life force isn't here. All you'd have is an empty body. And even if you did bring him back all the way, it wouldn't matter. He's already sacrificed himself. Bringing him back will just make him alive and in charge of gods know how many insane naga ghosts."

"Will you just trust me on this? Bring him back. I'm not going to let him be some kind of martyr for a race that hasn't been alive for a hundred million years."

"Actually –," Asklepiós began.

"I don't care how long ago it really was! Just do it."

Another tremor threw me into him. Samedi caught Beth and held her tight, causing her to slap him hard enough to leave a momentary handprint. Large cracks popped their way up the Damnation Lock.

"What I was about to say," Asklepiós said, pushing me away, "was doing that would...nevermind. It is unimportant. Come, Baron. I'll need your assistance."

"Come on, Beth," I said. "We've got an undead sea serpent to talk to."

"Please," she said, crossing her arms.

"End of the world here. Do I really need to be polite?"

"You do if you want my help."

"How do you know I want your help?" I asked. "Maybe I just want to get you away from Samedi's gropey hands."

"'Cause Mama Rosa knows what you're up to, Roger," Rosa croaked. "You're thinking 'bout the stories, like Asklepiós told you to."

"Never tell him that. Now, please, let's go save the world."

We ran. Well, Beth ran. I almost kept up at a brisk jog.

"You're getting a gym membership if we get out of this," Beth said back to me.

"I get it! I'm out of shape. Would you people please stop pointing that out?"

"Detective," Hitara said in my brain when we came through her jaws. "Rosa. You've come back."

"How old are you?" I asked Mama Rosa, not for the first time.

"Now, you know better than to go asking a girl her age," Rosa said.

"You have failed," Hitara said. "The cowardly dead are rising from the depths of Sraatsa."

"Not yet they're not," I said. "And they won't if you help me."

"You are requesting a boon from me? Are you truly that desperate, Detective? Think on this carefully. Favors —"

"From gods are bad, bad things," I finished. "I know the drill. They're still better than a horde of dead nagas ruling a dead world."

"Ask me your boon, then."

"Wake up Rohrons and have him drag Damballa's life energy up here and toss it in his body. And don't tell me you can't or he can't. Just about every pantheon ever is as inbred as a mountainful of hillbillies, and I doubt yours is any different. Blood calls to blood. Rohrons is your son, and I'm guessing Damballa is his, what, nephew?"

A crash like thunder echoed through the cavern, followed by a pulse of yellow energy lighting up the amber walls. Within them, thousands of shapes began to stir.

"Half-brother. His father was —"

"Right now, I don't care."

Green fires flashed in Hitara's eyes.

"No offense," I said quickly. "Just in a bit of a rush."

The fires dimmed, but still flickered. "This may take some time. Rohrons is in the deepest parts of Sraatsa, where the tides of belief from the damned are the strongest."

"Then get started. Time's about to run out."

Her eyes vanished from their sockets, leaving two dark holes and a skeleton that now seemed just that, a pile of long dead bones.

"Is she going to find him in time?" I asked Beth.

"I hope so. I'm not looking forward to fighting off another army of the damned."

I rolled my eyes. "I knew you still blamed me for that. First off, it wasn't an army; it was a regiment at the most. And second, it wasn't my fault. It was that moron with…wait, you hope so? Rosa can't see what's coming up?"

"No. There are too many strong possibilities. It's like looking at a TV screen showing four stations at once. There is one thing that all of them have in common, though."

"What's that?"

She smiled evilly. "Running."

"Great. Just what I wanted to hear."

Then came a crack like the world breaking, rattling my bones and sending shivers through my whole body. Over Hitara's skull, I saw the Damnation Lock shudder in resonance with the now continuous trembling coming up from the ground. Then, like someone had hit it with a wrecking ball, it exploded in a spray of shards.

I had just enough time to grab Beth and push her to the ground beneath me.

"Shit," I said as fragments of amber rained down on us.

"Please tell me that thing wasn't part of your big plan," Beth said.

"If you've got another way to sacrifice Damballa and close this Armageddon down, then I'm all ears."

"That's your plan? Re-sacrifice Damballa?"

"It'll work. Well, it would've…"

Beth pushed me off of herself and got up. She cocked her head, listening to Mama Rosa. "Rosa says there's an alternative."

I stood up and brushed amber off of myself. "Let me guess – we sacrifice someone else a little less disposable to us."

Hitara's eyes flared up. "You are in luck, Detective. My son comes."

"That was fast," I said.

"Danaido's presence here disturbed him. He was already on his way up to investigate. I asked him not to kill you."

"Thanks. All right, let's go," I told Beth, grabbing her hand and heading for the ruins of the Damnation Lock. Then, over my shoulder, "Please."

"What did you do?" Samedi asked as soon as we came out into the open, pointing his walking stick at me. "Dere's something mighty awful coming up from under us, Detective."

"It's on our side, for the most part," I said. "What's wrong with Asklepiós?"

Sitting with his back to Damballa's whole and healthy body, Asklepiós looked like he was a gentle breeze from falling over. He also looked to be about a hundred. His bronze skin was nearly white, his black hair had gone silver, and he had more wrinkles than my wardrobe.

"Did he use up all of his belief energy?" I asked. Then, to Asklepiós, "Did you?"

He managed a smile. "You do know that resurrecting a god isn't as easy as it sounds."

Beth ran up to him. "He doesn't have much time left, Roger."

"He's got enough, hon," Rosa said aloud.

"That's what Beth was talking about," I said. "Sacrificing him."

Beth's body aged as Rosa came fully forward. "Yes. Soon as that monster Rohrons brings Damballa back on up here, have the baron toss his butt back where it belongs. Then Asklepiós can do what he's gotta to stop this nonsense."

She looked down on the god and stroked his hair like she would a favorite grandson's. "I'm sorry, hon. There ain't no other way out of this. But you knew that."

He nodded and picked up my obsidian dagger by its rag sheathe. "Of course. I rather hoped for it, to be honest. It has been centuries since I've gotten to sacrifice myself for someone else."

If he said anything else, it was lost in the din of, as far as I could tell, every creature in existence screaming from below us. Even Samedi had to cover his ears. A waterspout of amber energy and blinding pain erupted from the remains of the Damnation Lock, sending me to my knees with black spots flaring across my vision. Soul upon soul whipped into a contained plasma of damned spirits, swirled about so fast that only a quick eye could catch the occasional tortured face as screaming spirit blended into screaming spirit. This was the diamond of sheer spiritual pressure that I hoped Asylum Tower's coal never turned into.

From out of its base stepped an old fisherman, complete with black, rubber hip-waders and a floppy hat covered in colorful trout lures. He even had an old wooden pipe sticking out of the steel grey beard covering his face. The only things spoiling the likeness were an amber gaff hook hung across his back and a woven net containing a blob of shifting spiritual energy slung across his shoulder.

The soul fountain receded, taking the noise and pain with it.

"Rohrons?" I asked after the ringing in my ears and the pain in my head had died down some.

He threw the net at Samedi's feet.

"Yours," he rasped, giving the s a little bit of a whistle, like it was hard for him to pronounce. "Him to take and this to stop."

"Are you just going to watch the fun?" I asked, wobbling to my feet. "Or is there anything you can do to help?"

Then all Hell broke loose. Literally. The ground heaved one last time, like it was trying to shake us off, then went still. Until every surface of the cavern sprouted clawed, scaly hands, which began dragging thousands of hungry, insane nagas out of their sixty-some odd million year prison.

Rohrons gave me a wink, revealing a golden, u-shaped iris upon opening. The pipe disappeared into a decidedly beak-like mouth. "The cowardly dead to remind of their eternal lord."

The ancient god unfolded and unfolded, seven tentacles pulling away from his body and lashing out in all directions, reaching impossible distances to strike the walls, and the eighth taking hold of the growing gaff hook and stabbing it into a wall. His head billowed out like a hot air balloon inflating, deforming it into a bulbous, fleshy thing and melting it into his chest. Iridescent yellow coloring flashed across his skin and turquoise circles erupted across it.

"This to stop," he repeated before pulling his monstrous body into the air and launching it at one of the walls.

I helped Asklepiós to his feet and walked him away from Damballa's body. It wouldn't do us any good if Damballa crushed him when he woke up back in his body.

"All right, you heard the giant octopus god," I said. "Let's stop this. You're up, Samedi."

Baron Samedi picked up the net containing Damballa's essence like it was the world's biggest dirty diaper, using only his thumb and forefinger and holding it as far away from himself as he could. "Time to be putting your skin on again, Brother. Ain't none of us likes seeing you naked like dis."

Samedi walked up to Damballa's head and dropped the net and its contents on it. With more flourish than was probably necessary, he raised his walking stick, twirled it around, and sliced open the net with its point. "Out and in with you."

The pulsing energy seemed to debate its options for a moment, rising slightly, then sinking back down and rolling a short ways down the snake's spine.

"None of dat, now," Samedi said, giving the god a solid smack with his walking stick. "Get back in your body."

Reluctantly, the energy sank into Damballa's skull. The slit pupils widened and the god rose up impossibly fast. But Samedi was faster. He leapt onto Damballa's head and began beating on it with his walking stick.

"YOU WILL DIE TONIGHT. ALL OF YOU. I WILL EAT YOUR SOULS AND LET THEM DIGEST FOR CENTURIES."

"Yeah, yeah," I said. "You know how many times I've heard that?"

"Do what you gotta do, quick," Samedi shouted down to us as Damballa thrashed around, trying to shake him off. "Dis ain't as easy as I make it look."

"You ready for this?" I asked Asklepiós.

He nodded.

I reached for my obsidian dagger, but he knocked my hand away.

"I have to do this myself," he said. "Just like Damballa did."

Asklepiós pulled the dagger from its sheath, revealing a blade so sharp and black that it seemed to be asking to slice through flesh. Any flesh, so long as it was warm and alive.

"Any last words?" I asked. "And please don't give me a prophecy. I hate those things."

He smiled, just a little. "Advice, then. When I do it, drop me and run, or whatever it is you do, Detective. Do not even look back, or Damballa will catch you."

"I'll do my best," I said.

And, without any further ceremony, Asklepiós reached up and slit his own throat. Blood spurted out in warm, pulsing streams, splashing my trench coat and shoes with red as he collapsed.

"Run, damn you," he mouthed as the light dimmed from his eyes.

"Time to go," I said to Beth, grabbing her hand and running away as fast as I could.

"What are you doing?" she asked, keeping up without any trouble. "You know that I'm going to be pulling that squishy thing you call a body by the end of this."

"Fine, just so long as we make it that far."

Before entering the corridor out, I yelled, "Keep him busy until we get out of the cavern, Samedi!"

"You best be fast, then," Samedi shouted back. "He's a feisty one when after a good resurrecting."

"RUN, SPIRITUALIST. THE PANIC WILL SWEETEN YOUR FLESH."

"He's such a sweet talker," I said as I ran. "Makes you wonder why there isn't a Mrs. Big Ugly Snake God."

"Shut up and run faster," Beth told me.

I made the mistake of looking up when we ran through Hitara's jaws. Directly above was something out of a surrealist's nightmares. Rohrons, covered in screaming nagas, was crawling over cavern walls as if gravity didn't matter to him. His tree-sized tentacles moved so fast I could barely see them, swiping across the walls to grab any naga who tried to escape its prison. When an arm had enough spirits attached to it, he'd loop it back to the serrated beak on his underside and devour them all. Every now and then, a particular spirit would enrage him and he'd spear it with the gaff hook. He was doing a great job of keeping them occupied, but he couldn't possibly keep up with the damned nagas. For every one he ate, three would pull themselves free and join their fellow damned in attacking him. For now, they couldn't do much damage to him, but gods only knew what would happen when enough of them ganged up on him and started taking chunks out of him. Insane spirits powered by the flesh of a god just seemed like something that would end poorly.

"Why are they still coming out?" I asked through the copper taste that was forming in my mouth.

"Asklepiós hasn't died yet," Beth said. "Give it a second."

On cue, a pulse of golden light swept through the cavern. The ground rumbled under us, and a glance behind me showed the Damnation Lock reassembling itself piece by piece, rising high into the cavern, sealing the damned in their prison again. Nagas pulling themselves out found themselves stuck in the amber like it was tar, bringing out the frustrated screams of thousands of dead, who, after a glimmer of hope, had it yanked away. Slowly, the walls sucked them into their depths, where they'd hopefully spend the rest of eternity. Able to focus on them now, Rohrons began sweeping the nagas hacking away at him into his cavernous beak.

"Don't gawk!" Beth ordered. "Run!"

We made it three-quarters of the way to the tunnel when I heard Samedi shout, "He's all yours, Detective!"

The ground rumbled beneath us. I didn't need to look back to know that Damballa was chasing at top speed.

"The tunnel should slow him down," I gasped to Beth, winded from way more exertion than I was used to. "That'll give us time to at least get to the ghost jungle."

"And then what?"

"Hopefully the dinosaur jumps on him while we get away. It's there to protect this place, so it should attack anything that comes through. It attacked you, didn't it?"

Beth shook her head. "No. The nagas that had me knew a word that let them get through."

"Swell. Maybe we'll get lucky and Damballa'll be too pissed to remember it."

The crashing behind us got closer.

"And I might be the king of Faerie," I said under my breath.

"Little brother to stay," Rohrons said. His gaff hook dropped out of the sky, smashing into the path behind us and destroying it. "I long was to away. We to…talk."

"Do you think –" I began.

"No," Beth said. "Damballa just has to squirm his way into this tunnel and Rohrons can't touch him. He might have bought us five minutes."

I expected that answer, but one can always hope that the universe only allows a certain amount of horrifying events to happen to someone within a given space of time. Apparently, I hadn't found that saturation point yet.

We got about halfway through the tunnel when the rumbling resumed.

"Or maybe two minutes," Beth said, picking up the pace. I managed to keep up, but a stitch in my side was beginning to shoot pain across my gut. I wouldn't be able to make it much longer.

We broke out into the jungle and leapt to the left side of the tunnel's opening as Damballa dove for us. There was a loud snap as his maw closed on empty air. He'd shrunk down enough to fit into the passages, but he was still several tons of pissed off snake god barreling out at us. The roars of several dinosaurs came from the jungle.

"Follow… the edge of the cave," I told Beth. I was almost wheezing now. "We'll try to circle… around to the other tunnel. We might… be able to get to it before he finds us."

We ran as fast as my exhausted body would allow.

"YOU CANNOT HIDE FROM ME! I WILL FIND YOU AND CONSUME YOU, SPIRITUALIST!"

Apparently, my luck had changed, because Damballa roared in pain, then said, "PATHETIC CREATURE. YOU ARE NOTHING."

There were several more roars from the dinosaur ghost, interspersed with the loud snap of Damballa's jaws. When we got to the tunnel's opening, I risked a look back. I was just in time to see him wrap his mouth around the tyrannosaur and begin to swallow it.

"Damn," I said.

"It'll keep him busy. Come on, we've got to keep moving," Beth said desperately.

But that wasn't what I was swearing about. I'd just seen our chance to beat Damballa.

I guessed we were about three-quarters of the way to the guardian when Damballa started smashing his way through the tunnel behind us.

"I…hope…the guardian…puts up a…better fight…than the dinosaur," I gasped, clutching the developing cramp in my side.

"I'm getting you a gym membership if we make it out of this," Beth said once again as she tried not to pull too far ahead. "You shouldn't be this out of shape."

"I'd rather…have the big snake…eat me."

We made it to the guardian's chamber with Damballa not twenty feet behind us.

The guardian, sitting on the pool and playing with my old lighter, looked up at us and growled.

"Go get 'im," I wheezed at the guardian as we went to the right along the chamber's edge.

Damballa shot out of the tunnel like a snake in a joke can and crashed into the guardian. It clawed at Damballa's right eye, blinding it and sending blood and vitreous humor spraying out. The god screamed.

"ROHRONS, YOUR GUARDIAN WILL SOON BE JOINING YOU."

The guardian didn't seem to like Damballa insulting its boss because it hulked out to its giant form and began furiously tearing into the blinded eye even more, splattering blood and gore everywhere. Damballa shook his head to no effect. The last thing I saw as we entered the final leg of tunnels was Damballa growing to match the guardian's size and beating it against the chamber's walls in an attempt to get it to let go.

"We're almost out, Roger," Beth said. "Come on."

Somehow, from the depths of whatever lived where my soul had left its "Dear Roger" note, I managed to get enough strength to go the last little bit to the Evil House's cellar. Once there, though, I stumbled over to the exposed secret room, skidding to a stop on the torn papers scattered about it.

"What are you doing?" Beth nearly screamed. "He'll be here any time!"

"I...know. Come over here. We...need to stay here and fight. There...isn't enough space...for him to move much. It's our...only chance."

"What are we going to fight him with? All we've got is the ankh." She held it up to me.

I shook my head. "Samedi's cane is...stuck in his head. We can use... it to kill him. It's a god's weapon."

The ground rumbled, like a volcano was about to erupt under us.

"YOU CANNOT ESCAPE ME, SPIRITUALIST!" came from underground.

Beth walked over to me. "You'd better be right."

"Or what?" I said with a smile. "You'll kill me?"

We only had to wait a minute. Damballa shattered the remains of the furnace and exploded through the first floor of the Evil House, sending dust and fragments of wood raining down on us.

I shook my head. "I called him smart once, didn't I?

"We're down here!" I shouted to the ceiling.

Damballa pulled himself back into the basement until he was looking at us with his good eye. Samedi's cane stuck out of his head just above it.

"GODS WILL SHAKE WHEN THEY HEAR ABOUT HOW YOU WILL SUFFER."

I jumped forward, grabbed the cane, and moved off to Damballa's right. The god hissed and swung around, attempting to follow me. Beth walloped him in the side when he did so, and he turned back to her.

I held the cane up to the height of Damballa's eye. "Hey, scaly, over here."

AMBER SEA OF THE DEAD

When the god turned upon hearing the focus of his rage, the force of his own momentum drove the cane through the gouged out eye and into his brain.

It also knocked me hard into the basement wall, causing everything to go black.

## 8.

The first thing I saw was a bright light.

"I'm finally dead, aren't I?" Part of me was kind of happy at the prospect. I'd had just about enough of giant octopus gods running around and giant snake gods chasing me down to eat me.

"No, you're not that lucky," Beth said from my right side.

The world came into a little more focus and I realized that I was in a hospital room. The bright light I was seeing was sunlight coming in through the windows behind her.

"You know, you almost look like an angel with all the light coming from behind you," I said.

She smiled. "But it takes more than that to fool you, right?"

"Damn straight. I've met too many angels. And I'm the guy who saved the world. Again. With almost no sleep, and for no money."

"With a lot of help," Beth added.

I tried to laugh, but my ribs hurt too much. I managed an "ouch."

"That hit from Damballa bruised your ribs, and your back is the second biggest bruise I've ever seen, so don't try anything strenuous soon."

I tried to laugh again, winced at the pain, and swore. "You know me better than that. The most strenuous thing I do if I can help it is leap a pile of garbage in my apartment."

"You do know that you could just burn strong incense to keep the ghosts out, don't you?"

"What, and ruin the atmosphere I've got going in there?" I said. "Besides, I couldn't evict all of those critters that are living in there now."

"You didn't know, did you?"

"No," I said quietly. "Guess I'll just have to get a new apartment and let the landlord clean out that one. Hope he brings a flame-thrower."

"This isn't our date, by the way."

"Damn," I said with fake anger.

Gingerly, I sat up in bed. Beth tried not to look concerned and, for the most part, was successful. For the first time, I saw that I only had on a blue hospital gown.

"I'm mostly naked here, aren't I?" I asked once I was sitting up all the way.

"Mostly," she replied. "Don't worry, I didn't look."

"But you were tempted," I teased.

"Out of morbid curiosity."

"How long was I out?"

"Just a day. The doctor said he was amazed that you were even still alive with all of the crap he found floating in your system when he did your blood-work."

I shrugged, then gasped at the stabbing pain. "We all have to die of something. I figure I might as well die of bad eating."

"Damballa almost took that little dream away. You were lucky."

"Luck my ass. There's a reason I don't exercise: Fat makes a better shock absorber than muscle."

"Whatever."

"At least I finally got to catch up on my sleep."

"I never took you to be an optimist," Beth said. "Are you sure you're okay?"

"It'll wear off. I'll be back to my old bitter and cynical self in no time."

"I can't wait," she said flatly.

"So what happened to Damballa?" I asked, ignoring the last comment. "I can't imagine his body just disappearing. And it's gotta be damn hard to hide a snake the size of most buildings."

"Samedi took care of it. Some god thing, I guess. He said he'd save you enough skin to make a pair of boots, and that you two were even if he could keep the body."

"Bullshit. If he keeps the body, he owes me, and I'm going to tell him the next time I see his rum-soaked ass. It's not every day that a god dies, unfortunately." Not that Damballa was permanently dead. He still had more than enough followers to come back, but it'd definitely be a few years until I had to worry about him again.

Which made me remember the god we'd left behind.

"Any word on Asklepiós?" I asked.

Beth shook her head. "No, but that doesn't mean anything. He could come back anytime."

Preferring to believe the little lie, I just nodded. We both knew he'd been on his way out and that there was no coming back for him.

After a moment of uncomfortable silence, I looked around the room. "Are my clothes in that closet?" I asked, pointing to a door.

"That's the bathroom. Your clothes are over there," Beth pointed to another door.

"Can you get my trench coat? I seem to be bed-ridden."

"This is the only time you get to play that card with me," Beth said as she got up.

She opened the door, took out my trench coat, and brought it over to me.

"Thanks," I said as I looked through its pockets.

"Here he is." I pulled out Chip's urinal cake.

"Our naga in college-kid's clothing, right?"

"Yeah. He's going to be experiencing things shortly that the Chinese don't have hells for."

Chip shook weakly.

"And I want my ankh back, by the way," I told Beth.

"It's in the Sunbird's glove compartment."

"Well take it out and put it somewhere safe. Kalamazoo's no New York, but there are still thieves here."

"Relax," Beth said. "It's safe."

I narrowed my eyes. "What did you do to my car?"

She smiled. "You'll just have to wait and see."

\*       \*       \*       \*

Eight hours later, I was deemed well enough physically to leave the hospital. My doctor still wasn't sure that he should let me go, muttering something about angioplasty, but he let me out anyway. With Beth's help, I hobbled out to the Sunbird. Sitting in its passenger seat was the guardian, playing with its lighter.

I bent down as best as I could and looked through the driver's-side window. "What is he doing here?"

"Funny thing. Damballa just beat him up and left him for dead, or whatever he would be. Turns out he was just knocked out."

I straightened up and looked across the Sunbird's roof to Beth. "And he wound up in my car how?"

Beth leaned on the roof. "Hitara's payment for helping you. She wanted him to have the chance to make up a little for Damballa. Besides, his pool got destroyed when he was fighting Damballa, and Samedi and a bunch of other death gods are sealing up the entrance to Sraatsa, so he doesn't have a home or a place to guard."

"So you thought that he could be the guardian of my car? Wouldn't a car alarm be better? I mean, he's...interesting and all, but I don't want to have to give him a lighter every time I want a friend of mine to ride along with me."

"I'll let you work that out with him."

"How?" I asked. "He doesn't speak English."

Beth started walking away. "You'll figure something out."

"Thanks. Hey, wait," I called after her. "Can you see him?"

"No," she said back to me. "He's a ghost up here."

I sighed. "Great. My own pet guardian ghost."

I opened the door and got in, slamming it behind myself. The guardian looked at me and growled.

"Oh shut up," I told him. "Play with your lighter."

# Epilogue

A week later, Beth and I sat at a table in a dimly lit corner of a restaurant. The smell of garlic drifted through the air, permeating everything.

"Is there a reason you wanted to go to an Italian restaurant?" Beth asked. She was dressed in a black, strapless dress that revealed more of her skin than I'd ever seen.

"Because there is no chance of work interfering with us here," I replied. I was wearing a grey, button-up shirt and black slacks. "The garlic will keep away everything except –"

"Roger!" a familiar voice shouted across the dining room.

I looked down and put my fingers on my temple. "I really hate him sometimes."

"We're off the clock," Beth yelled back at Samedi. "Come back tomorrow."

"Don't tell anyone I said this, but I think of the two of you as gods. And gods, we're never off the clock."

"Would you stop shouting and get over here?" I yelled over to Samedi, who was leisurely making his way over, soaking up the stares of the other customers and the waitstaff.

Samedi pulled out a chair when he reached our table and sat. "I haven't seen you two since the big nastiness with my brother. I was concerned."

I raised an eyebrow. "That'd be a first."

The god clutched his heart. "You hurt me, Detective. I've always had nothing but your best interest in my heart."

"You don't have a heart," Beth said flatly.

"Ah, but if I did, it would have your best interest in it."

"We're in the middle of a date here, Samedi," I said. "Could you just cut to the chase and tell us what you want?"

"Of course. I wanted to know where you got that wonderful rum of yours. You promised you would tell me who was giving it to you."

"That was before you carved up Damballa for steak."

"I gave you a lovely pair of boots I had made special from his skin. They'll never wear out."

"They're cowboy boots!" I shouted.

Beth laughed, trying unsuccessfully to hide it behind her hand.

I pointed a finger at her. "Don't encourage him."

"She's a beautiful woman, Detective, who knows a good pair of boots when she sees one."

"And who isn't affected by lusty gods," Beth added.

"Go away, Samedi," I told him. "I don't owe you anything, and you know it."

"You can't blame me for trying, can you?"

I shook my head. "No, but I'm about to. Now get."

"I don't know. They seem to have a wonderful selection of wine in this place."

"Boy, if you don' git on outta here, I'm gonna tell these two how to put you in a bottle an' toss you into Lake Michigan," Mama Rosa said to Samedi.

"You don't know how to, old woman," the god told her.

"You're cute as all hell, but don't tempt me, child."

Samedi considered this for about two seconds, then stood up and bowed slightly. "Enjoy your date, my friends. I will see you soon enough."

"Gods I hope not," I said, smiling.

Samedi walked away, but before he could get far, I said to him, "Thanks for your help with Damballa. You didn't have to, but you did anyway. I appreciate it. Tell the ghosts, too. Hell, I might even leave Taylor alone for a while for helping out on this one."

The god turned and gave a deep bow. "You are most welcome, Detective, and I will." He turned back around and left.

"You know he probably did it just to get Damballa's body, don't you?" Beth asked.

"Yeah, but I'm inclined to give him the benefit of the doubt, if just for today. Apparently I'm a lot more chipper when I'm rested."

"Roger?" a voice I hadn't heard in years said from where Samedi had just left, causing my heart and stomach to switch places. "Bob said you needed help with something."

I turned. "Delilah?"

# JASON ARBOGAST

www.ingramcontent.com/pod-product-compliance
Lightning Source LLC
Chambersburg PA
CBHW070549180626
46817CB00005B/1750